Halve It

Joe Nasta

BLUE FORGE PRESS
Port Orchard ✹ Washington

Blue Forge Press is the print division of the volunteer-run, federal 501(c)3 nonprofit, Blue Legacy (EIN 83-4307421), founded in 1989 and dedicated to supporting artisans marginalized due to race, age, disability, economics or other factors. We strive to empower storytellers from all walks of life with our four divisions: Blue Forge Press, Blue Forge Films, Blue Forge Gaming, and Blue Forge Sound. Find out more at www.BlueForgeGroup.org

Blue Forge Press
7419 Ebbert Drive Southeast
Port Orchard, Washington 98367
blueforgepress@gmail.com
360-550-2071 ph.txt

Table of Contents

Halve It

Joe Nasta

The Winner

The carcass caught the highbeams. Not flattened. Not dead on impact. The trauma slowly spread from her skin to her innards. There wasn't even blood, and if it weren't for the rank stench wafting in the nighttime cool like a dense grenade stink bomb Chuck and Derek wouldn't have even known she wasn't alive.

Deer, flashlight, axe. He won a dollar.

He always started with one—a *Deep Woods* pull tab—and always bought more if it scratched his itch. Derek salivated at the thrill of tiny sinful victories.

"Three on Two, Two on Three, and One on Five?" Jerry asked behind the bar, cocked strawberry blonde. He knew the ritual. "And a Manny's?"

Every Tuesday afternoon, Derek sauntered in from the bright sidewalk so only the buzz of neon signs struck through the dim as he hunched on his stool. Bud light, Bacardi, and a Seattle Mariner's compass were his favorite ones to sit under so blue and red lights scrawled on Jerry's chalky teeth when he smiled.

HALVE IT

"Iii klsdlfkaskaslkd." He mumbled something in return and pulled the exact amount of cash from his pocket. It was a deer, for sure, Chuck had gotten out and checked. Anyway, it was four decades ago; they had been fifteen, sixteen. Derek relaxed and grinned at the bartender's blue eyes before reaching for his pile of lottery tickets.

Peeling back the bit of cardboard on the tabs to reveal three cartoon-like images was even more satisfying than cranking a slot machine lever. It picked a particular scab inside his chest, got his blood flowing. When a red line with a prize amount appeared on top of the pictures, a bit of bile rose in his throat. The first set was called *Hot Wings*: A peanut, a baseball, a stern mustached man. A bat, a chicken, and something unspeakably red. A hot rod, french fries, a drumstick.

No red lines. Three losses. He threw them into the red gingham picnic container meant for bar peanut shells and spent pull tabs.

They went to the baseball game the day after. Didn't talk about the accident, or what went down in the truckbed with the Glad garbage bags, by the Carson family's red mailbox at two a. m., back at the cabin in the top bunk.

The bleachers burnt Derek's hands when he sat on them. Chuck inspected the home team's slugger swing in double-knit polyester and striped pants while he cracked a peanut shell, popped the salty morsel into his mouth. His forearms and biceps strained with the cracking sound of a moonshot, and the player's cleats kicked dirt up towards the too-blue sky on his ceremonial run around the bases.

Derek wanted to remember, so he watched Chuck and

thought about the deer's fur.

A pool shark broke on the table behind Derek, clattering the balls across the green velvet. He shook his head. He felt embarrassed when he lost, in case Jerry was watching while he began to peel open *Pirates Plunder*. Rogue wave. Jolly Roger. Gold dubloon. Eye patch. Treasure chest. Turquiose squid. No prize.

In the middle of the night the boys snuck down to the lake, just the two of them. Chuck's idea, of course. Derek was always following him around. There weren't any clouds to hide the quarter moon's shine magnified by the water's reflection. The woods on the far shore were the only dark, and that is where Chuck wanted to go.

He gulped from the frosted glass. The cold in his chest was refreshing. It spread from his throat to his abdomen, soothing. It was an issue of focus: He could never pay attention to the right things, and the important details missed him, followed by a choice to forget.

When jumped in, the water was warm still from the scorching August heat even though the night had chilled the air. Chuck went first, pencil dropping with hardly a splash. "C'mon, let's swim over," his bobbing head laugh-whispered.

It was two of the regulars at the pool table, but he didn't remember their names or faces. He liked their hands, the different ways their fingers balanced and manipulated the cue stick. The one with thicker fingers and calloused thumbs chalked and lined up a shot for number two, solid blue, but the angle was slightly off and it went astray of the corner pocket.

Derek was sloppier when he entered the lake. Clumsy, he

hit it wrong and made a loud smacking sound. What if someone had heard them? The second after impact the heat from the water covered his face as he sank like a rock, fingers holding closed nostrils. Count to three, opened eyes. Chuck was already breast-stroking away. He emerged above the water and took a deep breath of air before he followed the boy into the dark.

The final pull tab lay in front of him on the bar. *Red White and Win.* He held it in his right hand, tempting a paper cut with his thin skin, wanting to bleed. The fireworks, three bursts in a row. The regular with more delicate hands aimed a bank shot for red-striped 11. First one thud on the rail, and a clunk as the shot sank in.

"We've got a winner!" He wished that Jerry had been watching after all and he would beam at him, finally. Derek would feel that warmth for the first time in years as his favorite bartender crossed the last $500 off the sign with a thick permanent marker. Imagine!

The rest of the memory waterlogged the unbraided threads of the rope swing and the scrape of dry bark on his footsoles. There was an aftertaste of clean lake water, salted flesh, milk breath. Jerry was busy at the other end of the bar serving a couple of handsome twenty-five year olds, tracing their outlines as he shot Coke from the soda gun into a glass. The itch tore open across his chest and his want became too much to bear.

Pathetic. Even winning was not enough. Derek chugged the rest of his beer and threw the unredeemed pull tab away.

Welcome to the Sunrise Suites

The stray dog always returned. He lay in the shadows cast by the palm trees and the motel's vacancy sign. Every afternoon around 3 pm the scraggly boy came by for his nap because the concierge left a bowl of water and some kibble. She'd even supplied him with an oversized T-shirt to protect his skin from the dirt and sun: *Someone in Palm Springs, California is thinking of me* was emblazoned across his back.

The lobby's white tile tinted in the yellow light streaming in the cigarette-stained upper panels of the windows. Midafternoon sun slowed each August in the throat of the desert's hourglass. Behind the counter, the attentive boredom of the offseason coiled and twisted in the concierge's chest like a spring about to snap. Her second-hand Prius sat in one corner of the nearly empty parking lot with a Snoopy-themed heat screen in the windshield. She recognized the same beige color of her car in the couch's upholstery and the stray dog's fur.

HALVE IT

Each morning before her shift, the concierge dotted her pale nose with freckles using a makeup pencil and pulled back her red hair before donning a bellboy's hat she'd found collecting dust in a maintenance closet. She enjoyed making herself up, applying a clear lip gloss, performing small rituals as if somebody were watching through the wide windows of the motel. She folded the freshly laundered linens. She sprayed blue glass cleaner on the mirrors and wiped the foam away with a cotton rag in widening spirals. She swept sand from the entryway intensely.

Now, she was investigating. The concierge typed, "California serial killer," "escaped convict," and "handsome mugshot news" into a search engine on the check-in computer and took notes in cursive on bright yellow post-its. Several guests had reported their encounters with a hitchhiker on their way into town, but none had stopped to pick him up. Mrs. Dillinger in room 203 mentioned his piercing green eyes when she checked in last night. The speedo-clad couple in 114 were fans of the hitchhiker's colorful, thick-lined tattoos and sleeveless white undershirt. They were all clearly enamored by his good looks, but she'd worked here long enough to know that beautiful things in the desert were usually poisonous.

On the edge of the property, the hitchhiker wrapped his body around a palm tree. Its rough skin caught the inside of his elbows like velcro. The bark pinched until it loosened from the inner layers of wood, exposing them like the red lines of tender its coarse fingernails left along his veiny forearms. Determined to get the best view of the oncoming traffic and potential rides, he wrapped his Levi-clad legs around the trunk and shimmied upwards.

That's when he saw the crimson Cadillac. Chrome detailing sparkled and burned his eyes as the car slowed at the entry to the parking lot. He couldn't believe his luck. The dog raised its ears as it passed but left his eyes closed. The hitchhiker squinted, the edges of his lips curling. The window tint was too dark to be legal so he couldn't be sure the driver was, but he imagined a blonde with a strong jaw like River Phoenix. He licked his lips. But the waistband of his blue jeans started to slip off of his hips and he knew he was going to fall before the sudden whir of air—a few seconds of weightful bliss until he hit the ground.

Emily kept the curtains closed in her room to ward off the heat, only relieved every few hours by a cold shower. It had been dumb to come this time of year but she'd needed an escape from her three kids and malingering husband, the work-from-home freelance job that dangled a promotion over her head but never delivered. It was time to relax and she deserved it.

She turned the shower faucet off, stepped toe first onto the cool tile, and reached for the orange terry cloth bathrobe instead of the towel; she'd rather stay damp than rub herself dry because it felt more luxurious. She sat on the edge of the bed directly in front of the fan with the robe untied. Soaked strand of straight brown hair flattened against her cheeks.

A thud outside the door.

"Who's there?" she called out wearily. No use opening the door to let the AC out. The response sounded somewhere between a dog's whimper and a cracking branch. None of Emily's concern. She squinted, sighed, and fell back onto the gray comforter.

HALVE IT

By the pool, the couple were enjoying their first vacation together. When Aaron stepped out of his Birkenstock, his heel and toes burned. The high-pitched buzz of the desert continued.

"If you're not in the water before I count to—"

"Hot! Hot!" he cut Steve off as he hopped across the cement until he reached the edge.

No wind broke the surface of the swimming pool but it moved gently, playing coy with the white lines of sunlight. Heat became too unbearable between Aaron's shoulder blades as he lowered a foot down the ladder's top rung, the ribbed rubber casing digging into her sole. Relief soothed his skin as first one foot & then the other breached the clear blue, sending circles towards the center of the pool.

"But it's too cold to go under!" Steve grabbed both of his ankles with his wet hands, ran them up and down Aaron's bare legs. The faint hair on the front of his hamstrings stood on end, then he fell backwards with a splash on top of his lover. They came up for air laughing.

The crashing sound of splattering water broke the concierge out of her reverie. She'd been developing an elaborate explanation for the handsome hitchhiker based on the plot of a crime TV show she'd seen the night before, but the sudden crash disturbed her. Must be that couple, she thought, they've been making loud thumping noises ever since they'd arrived. She stared dramatically towards the door to the pool deck with a brief idea of checking on them, then shook her head. The bell above the door rang as a new guest arrived. She smiled without missing a beat. "Welcome to the Sunrise Suites!"

Early the next morning the dog's insistent barking woke

her from a dream in which she was a private detective. She didn't bother to put pants on under her size XXL Harley Davidson T-shirt before slipping into her flip-flops and hastening to the source of the noise: The man from her dream unconscious under a palm tree. She was the first to arrive on the scene, but soon the exasperated woman emerged in the motel's bathrobe and the gay couple showed up in matching plaid pajama sets.

The dog's gentle tongue was not reviving the hitchhiker. The couple was right: The tight tank top and muscle tone was quite exciting to look at, even in this state. The concierge took a deep breath but savored the rush of blood to her head. Her daydreaming had prepared her for this moment.

A car door slammed and the ignition turned over with a roar. The hitchhiker opened his eyes and shot up just in time to see the blood red Cadillac stealing away, gold and white neon reflecting in its black windows.

Desire

The shrill alarm woke the groundskeeper—something near the gate to the property triggered the sensor. Miriam had only been half-asleep, so the sudden ringing shot right through her from the bottom of her feet to the loose bun of brown hair. Her chipping French pedicure poked out beneath the orange and brown quilt. What day was it? The Casio watch on her wrist said it was Monday, 2 a.m. The time passing had already become meaningless, but in a way she savored. No deadlines to meet and no social obligations. She'd not seen anybody for a week.

Miriam had the kind of year that led to a one-way ticket out of Seattle, a three-month contract as groundskeeper on a 72-acre clandestine estate in Southeast Alaska. She was still finding her way around, relying on an outdated hand-drawn map she found in the desk drawer of her cabin. The mysterious job posting she saw online, the irresistible pull towards a new life, and the crumbling of her old one were just a single blink as she wiped the last crust of sleepiness from her eyelids.

What struck her most about Alaska was the vastness.

HALVE IT

Everything was so far away from everything else but there never seemed to be a hard edge where the water ended or the forest emerged. As she disembarked from the ferry ramp onto the dock, the weight of her past was released and a giddy possibility emerged from her mouth; Miriam laughed. An ache planted in her sacrum: desire.

Diana, a lively elderly woman, picked her up in a rusted Chevy Blazer that she heard before it emerged around the corner, wet plumes of smoke puffing from the tailpipe. The woman glowed as the truck pulled up outside the Marine Highway terminal, unruly auburn curls framing her easy smile.

"Ever been to Sitka before?" The soft cadence of her voice invited Miriam into the passenger seat. The car door shut behind her with a satisfying slam.

"No, never even been to Alaska!" Her voice cracked. Diana turned the wheel and pulled onto the main road. The grey sky, trees, and black asphalt expanded endlessly.

"Ah, fresh meat. Don't worry, you'll be a pro in no time," She took her gleaming eyes off the road for a moment to glance across the car. Diana's skin was smooth as porcelain with a ruddy blush on her cheeks. After showing her the cabin, handing over the keys to a pickup truck, and wishing good luck, she left the new groundskeeper completely alone in the woods.

As Miriam powered up the laptop to check the gate's security camera feed, she didn't feel like a pro. A bolt of hyperaware tingling spread from the pit of her stomach up towards her neck, into the veins of her arms. The black and white night appeared on the screen, too bright for her eyes at first. She squinted, scanning the image for an intruder but then she saw the black-tailed stag. He lay directly in front of the gate with his antlers between the metal bars. A gash simmered on his right flank and blood oozed into a puddle in the dirt.

Her heart sank. There was no coming back from the injury. Miriam grabbed the handgun and a flashlight, slid into thick wool socks and slip-on shoes, and pulled a thick flannel coat over her shoulders. The wild creature's suffering weighed in her hips like lead.

Hyperaroused, she followed the flashlight beam on the short trail to the gate. She'd never shot anything living before but knew how to aim and pull the trigger. Gentle whimpers in the distance grew into loud cries ringing through the dark her vision hadn't adjusted to yet. It was much colder than during the day, causing her to shake violently and disturb the yellow stream of light.

She thought she remembered the way because of the split tree stump, moss spilling out of the inner rings like unoxygenated blood. Miriam hadn't found it, the source of the noise. Crack. It wasn't her fear that led her down the path, although she felt blood in her ears and a short circuit in her chest. It was her need to know, the ever-craving wonder of desire and a chainsaw pull. It was a dangerous wonder that made Miriam fumble her route and forget where the creek edge emerged.

The sudden ice cold shocked her and she let out a muffled shriek, pulling her foot out too quick. The shoe lodged under a rock and remained in the stream. She fell backward, blinding herself with the flashlight beam before dropping the torch. The whining grew louder, as if the wounded stag had disentangled itself from the gate to crawl, dragged itself along the damp earth following her wrong turns to the stream. The branches, charging antlers, scraped her face.

Flapping wings and yellow eyes of an owl swooped down before she could duck, its talons catching on her shoulder as she ran.

Wednesday was their last day in Alaska before returning home. "I've got a big one!" the father shouted, fishing pole in his hands. Eric wanted to show his preteen son this thrill on their first big trip together since the divorce as it would bother his ex-wife. However, Stevie sat on the edge of the stream pushing dirt around with a stick, completely disinterested. Maybe one day he would remember small glimpses of this day fondly, Eric hoped.

It wasn't his year for the holidays so he'd negotiated a few days of camping on his family's land near Sitka before the summer ended. It was where he had grown up, but he hadn't been up here since his mother died four years ago. It hurt too much to imagine her reddish-brown hair and comforting matriarchal smile in the home she built, so he contracted groundskeepers to keep miscreants away and generally occupy the small cabin near the entrance to the estate, maintaining the boundary of his private property. Eric often picked young women in search of change that reminded him of his mom's fierce spirit.

When the boys arrived on Monday afternoon, the groundskeeper never came to pick them up, so had to borrow a truck from someone in town and drive up the dirt road to the gate only to find a dead stag lying in a muddy pool of its own blood. The flies buzzed around the carcass.

After he and Stevie shoved the animal clear of the gate and drove in, Eric knocked on the cabin door to check in on the new steward of his land but there was no answer. This wasn't the first time a groundskeeper hadn't made it through their first week and left without a trace. Everyone thinks they want to get away from the world to live in the middle of the woods until they actually arrive and realize they're not cut out for it. He made a mental note to post a new job ad when he got back home next week.

"She's fighting but I feel it, about to lose!" He strained against the taut fishing line, reeling in until the resistance snapped and the hook went flying towards him. "Holy shit!"

On the end of his hook, he found a pink camo croc with a crescent moon jibbet.

"Wow, great catch Dad," Stevie quipped sarcastically.

"Well, at least we got a bit of trash out. What are we paying these groundskeepers for anyway if all they do is litter and abandon their post!"

His son laughed. "I would too if I were them!"

The owl cawed after Miriam as she fled completely blind. As the breaths tumbled up her chest, she heard drumming.

A figure emerged in a clearing filled with cascading amaranth, feathery crimson. Four deer with golden antlers encircled a woman who flicked her wrists. When trees around the clearing burst into flames, Miriam recognized her pale face and red-tinged hair. She nearly fell over as she panted, hunched over with her hands on her knees. Blood pounded in her ears.

"Diana?"

"Do not be afraid."

HALVE IT

"Diana!"

"Run into the flame."

The field was now surrounded by amber tongues of heat. Each deer contorted in the wavering light and shadows as their flesh collapsed, melted, reconstituted as human flesh: the former groundskeepers. The young women whispered and beat their chests in time with the pounding rhythm.

Aching want moved up her spine while blissful sensation spread into every corner of her body. Miriam knew: instinct. The new groundskeeper ran towards Diana's warm embrace, into the flame.

She was missing her right shoe, but the thick wool socks were still intact and the flannel was warm. The burning clearing, Diana, and deer-women were gone.

A car rushed by the shoulder of the highway, jolting Miriam with its high beams. The whirring sound of the passing cars was startling. Groggy, she propped her body up and blinked.

A copper scent lingered and the taste of dirt remained on her teeth. It was just past 10 p.m. on Friday according to her watch. The evening calm overtook her.

She pulled herself up from the ground, squinted at the green sign pointing toward town, and began to walk.

Hard at Work

You remember Alan, right? He didn't talk much. He moved from table to table around the bar. He picked up the beer glasses and soggy coasters, smiling coyly at the men who made eye contact or sticking out the tip of his tongue at the ones who didn't. Without speaking, he'd nod his head towards the empties, raise an eyebrow, barely part his pink lips.

Most of them ignored him, which he loved. He preferred to glide to the corners on the other side of the pool table with a cute but mysterious cloud around him, listening to the disparate snippets of conversation mixing with the songs from the jukebox.

Several unrecognizables and first-timers came in Fridays before the parties, DJs, and drag shows at Pony, R Place, or The Cuff started.

"And can you believe he kicked me out in the pouring rain? It was literally midnight! He could have at least called me an Uber!" a blonde with a chiseled jaw at the rail between the two pool tables beamed.

He thought he deserved more from the stud of the week he'd met on Grindr. Blondie threw his hands in the air to emphasize the point and show off how his biceps bulged under his mesh top.

On the other side of the rail, his mustachioed friend grimaced and nodded with a strained neck. "Um, yeah. I believe it. All the hot ones end up being dicks."

But the barback was on to the next group of pregamers before he could learn more details of the hookup gone wrong that had caused Blondie's disgust and dapper dude's nonchalance.

"Thank you!" Their heads followed him as he walked away.

Even though everyone used the phone app instead of walking over to the colorfully lit machine on the wall, Alan could tell who played what songs. Ed liked Meghan Trainor. Tommy got annoyed by what Ed played, so he paid extra to skip over those songs so there would be a few Madonna or Britneys in a row before an extrovert with a sterling silver ring on a chain around his neck played Beyoncé. He hadn't made a name up for him yet—and that was just the Thursday afternoon crowd before trivia.

Each day of the week had its regulars and he knew them all by the small details they shared as he bussed their tables and the almost imperceptible differences in their music tastes. Some preferred comfort, wore sweatpants that fit snug in the front and flip-flops that didn't hide their hairy toes. Others wore work clothes for a quick happy hour drink before returning home to their husbands and kids, some guys showed off designer bags and leather jackets, and transplants from Montana and Texas sported classic denim and cowboy boots. He preferred shorts, sneakers, and comfy sweatshirts like the one from Scotch and Soda's Looney Toons collection as he floated between them.

"Don't look, he's gonna notice," a pool shark who brought his own stick, chalk, and cue ball during the Wednesday tournament averted his vision from the bear at one of the hightops. His tequila soda had been empty for a few minutes too long and the ice was beginning to melt.

"But that's how the game is played," his curly-haired friend quipped with a half-full non-alcoholic beer.

With perfect timing, the bear in question gulped the last of his Manny's Pale Ale and wiped his hands on the hem of his polo shirt; all of the napkins on his table were soiled. Alan was delighted when he heard them talking about the twinks in the corner who avoided his gaze: a new whisper to carry. The cruising became the map of his shift when the customers were too busy fantasizing and ignoring each other to realize when their trash disappeared.

It was also his job to scrub the urinals. On slow nights like Tuesdays he did it periodically, one at a time between his rounds collecting dirty dishes. He slid the yellow rubber gloves up to the middle of his forearms and removed the bubblegum urinal cake after he poured two capfuls of pine sol into a bucket of scalding hot water. The earthy antiseptic scent with a hint of lemon bubbled against the stained porcelain after it was squeezed from the sponge, splattering into the cross of drain holes.

It was satisfying to wipe away the grime, leaving behind a sparkle. He enjoyed scrubbing, the stretch in his wrist tendons, and the soreness that built up in his fingertips. It gave him time to absorb all the rumors, desires, reflections he overheard from the lapping tongues that surrounded him. He imagined them running up his arms and legs, down the neck of his shirt as he plopped in a new urinal cake and washed his hands. Each whisper intertwined with another until they told the same stories of pain, anguish, lust, and laughter and became a shrill ring that conveyed nothing but raw emotion.

"Oh yeah, exactly like that," Jay said. The older man in flannel smiled earnestly at you, his pupil. "Focus, aim, and throw."

The two of you have been making your way to the back room dart boards every Monday for weeks. Alan thought you were an odd pair but he loved watching you learn the rules. This was back when you were still young, unsure, and alone in the city. You came down from the University District to order soda and popcorn, to play darts here with Jay.

Alan loitered down the steps, just beyond the threshold to the main bar and out of your periphery. Once you had caught him watching but didn't let on. He was like a stray cat weaving through the space collecting everyone's remnants. Now, he kept one eye on your Coke and the other on your dart.

You took a deep breath and gave your full attention to your body. It was as much about calming your mind as developing physical skill. You gripped lightly, pointed your elbow to the front of the room, planted your right foot forward like Jay had shown you. With the release, the dart shot true and landed just shy of the bull's eye.

"Amazing!" he said. "You've improved so much! Good

boy, you're doing so well." Then Alan came and brought you both a refill.

The barback had Sundays and Saturdays off, but that's none of your business. You didn't get to know about who he was outside of this place. Come to think of it, you haven't seen him in a while.

Exit 163

"oving?" The Uber driver asked once she saw the splayed pile of duffel bags and boxes. Meredith needed to load them into the trunk for the twenty minute ride.

"I guess. We broke up," she shrugged in the general direction of the gated townhome community behind her. Locked out of suburban paradise in the Renton Highlands, she'd return to her home in the city. At least the year of rent, utilities, WiFi payments she Venmoed to her housemates hadn't gone to waste, but the landlord had put his foot down and this was their last month living there, right when she was returning. They were going to tear part of it down, remodel, and build as many tall, skinny residential units they could fit on the lot. It was such a great location just two blocks from the Beacon Hill light rail so she understood why they wanted a more appealing option than her.

"I don't know if all that is going to fit."

Tonight she would go dancing at her favorite club to catch up with all the friends she hadn't seen in far too long. For the past year, Damien had preferred her by his side when he went bowling with his friends, played pool at his favorite bar, or hosted dinner parties with her homemade pumpkin soup on Halloween or her mom's recipe for rum-infused watermelon on the Fourth of July. Honestly, she was so excited to order takeout alone this Thanksgiving.

"I'd help you lift everything but I've got a bad back," Shirley the driver said, "I'll move these bags to the front seat so you have more room." Meredith plied her belongings gently into shape with the heels of her hands so they fit just right above the boxes of her books before shutting the trunk.

Shirley laughed. "I'm only driving in my retirement to fund my QVC habit," she shared as they pulled onto I-5 North. "You're lucky to have somewhere to go back to. But if you're ready to date again I know a guy; he's funny and has a husky but drinks a lot of beer."

"That's nice," Meredith smiled, making eye contact with her through the rearview mirror.

Freshly laundered, Damien's linen sheets smelled like home. He so rarely washed them, instead waiting for Meredith to strip the mattress and peel the cover off the duvet. For too long she fed her own want one pillowcase at a time in his laundry room with his liquid Tide and fabric softener. He wanted the washing machine's detergent drawer filled to the brim with the blue and green fluids, although she knew it killed the machine. Even when he wasn't watching she complied.

He got back from work to Meredith face down in the bed, sniffing. She wiggled her arms and splayed luxuriously in her favorite underwear to feel the smooth textures of the still warm sheets on her forearms, ankles, upper thighs, giggling at how sensitive she was.

"Baby, thank you for washing my linens, cleaning the bathroom, waiting for me," she imagined him cooing. " I love you in lace. Let me help you," she imagined him smirking.

He didn't say anything. Not even, "Hello, Darling."

That's when she made up her mind. She still made the bed before she left the next morning.

"He lives in a good trailer in a fifty-five and over community," the driver said. She used to bake cakes for weddings. She knew every venue in Seattle and the beginning of every ending. The skyline glistened as they approached Exit 163.

There wasn't a cloud in the sky but it was one of the first truly cold days, even this late in autumn. An imperceptible gust rustled the red leaves. As she unloaded all of her things on the the curb outside the wooden gate, the brass wind chime sang softly to welcome her.

Tonight it will feel like everyone in the room knows each other and she knows them too, but nobody will want to dance with her, speak to her. Maybe she should have texted to let them know she was coming or maybe she should have remembered their names, she'll think about every single person she recognizes. Do they remember her? The popping electronic music always blares too loud to speak and only the motions of hips convey meaning in the dark.

Tonight Meredith's arms will dissolve and she will evaporate, her wispy body lingering a foot and a half behind as she slithers between everyone in the club until she sees Damien in the corner alone. His sleek black hair will be slicked back with pomade. She'll smell the Old Spice from across the room.

The fog machine will go off above the dance floor and roving orange, red, yellow lasers cutting through the thick air in sharp lines will intersect the dancers' necks, exposed shoulders, abdomens between low rise belt loops and cropped T-shirts rising above belly buttons. When some arms reach up, some asses will drop, and Meredith will squint in what she hopes is the right direction searching for him in the crowded club.

Damien, some other guy, whoever. She won't do this again. Maybe there's only one more month in this house but her wind chime sounds arrhythmically even when she can't see what direction the air is moving. Her own laundry needs to be done and she will always love the people she loves. No matter what DJ is featured, their music will echo in her ears tonight but she'll keep dancing by herself. She swears there will be no more frantic searching for a handsome man who isn't hoping to be found in a flashing blur of pulsing music, wavering flesh, inexcusable desire.

"Good luck!" Shirley said as Meredith shut the car door a bit too forcefully, and then she drove away. One bag and box at a time she carried her things through the gate, across the overgrown lawn, up the steep porch steps, and into the only place she knew she could call home.

A Field Without You

inally, the dinner party was over.

The final guest rose from her seat in the chaise lounge as you lowered your eyes, stood in the corner of the condominium by the floor to ceiling glass that spanned the entire wall, and murmured, "Thank you, Denise. We both appreciated your company this evening," in an unconvincing tone. I did adore how insincere you became whenever an engagement lasted a few hours longer than expected.

We had just met her as a friend of a friend at a Sagittarrian astrologer's birthday dinner at the Pink Door. Denise glowed as she called the waiter over to order more red wine in front of the silk ribbons and aerial performers. She wrote poetry about desire, human flesh. When she read a poem dedicated to our mutual friend our heads turned, intrigued. In town for a short but indeterminate time, her mystery opened in front of us and we couldn't resist.

This was before the building across from our balcony was constructed and we could still smoke joints in our boxers with a view of the Bay, the Great Wheel, the Aqueduct demolition without feeling ashamed of the mirror: that duplicate tower filled with mismatched couples roaming minimally furnished rooms who became unhappier as the nights grew longer. This was before we couldn't stand each other.

Denise laughed. "Next time I won't open that extra bottle of wine." She shimmered in red sequins under the light from the piers and the night sky leaking into the dim room. You looked up from dropped eyelids with that irresistible smirk, silent. I showed her to the door. When it shut your hands at my waist startled me, your tongue on the ridge of my neck and your pecs on my shoulder blades delighted me. "Finally."

No longer. The end. What did you need from this? We both want different things.

When you called me last night and you said you missed me, did you think I would say yes? I said yes. You wanted me to come to you but I didn't. I stood up and said, "No, You Come Here For Once." And you did.

I don't want to leave you behind. We are here together. We will leave what we thought we wanted behind and rebuild.

What do we need from this? Locking eyes across the room, a small wave. A few minutes of conversation. What if we kissed on the corner? What if we kissed in the street? Denise glided through the cold night crosswalk twenty-four stories below.

The end. We can be what we want. Nobody needs to know. We need nothing. Finally, we were alone again. This was before we realized we couldn't stand each other.

The morning after I met up with Denise for lunch at a deli because she had a hankering for egg salad. "How was the rest of your night?" she asked with her coy smile. She always had a cloud of allure around her and her venomous red curls. "I'm so disappointed you didn't ask me to stay."

You were at work in your tech company's office in the Smith Tower, which loomed over the entire neighborhood like a beacon or a middle finger. From your desk you could look out the window and watch us walking around the neighborhood, miniatures and matchbox cars between the bare trees. I wanted you to see us when I grabbed Denise's hand. She squeezed back and laughed, throwing her head back. From every corner I felt the white terracotta tower pointing above us, enjoying feeling so small but so seen.

Only the first few floors of the skyscraper's wide base were made of granite, and the pointed tower was already almost inconsequential next to the taller glass columns rising out of downtown. But right here under your window when I let my hand drift to Denise's lower back and leaned in to kiss her neck your office building felt like the tallest building around. She moved her hands to the side of my neck.

What happened next? Finally, the end. It doesn't matter. I didn't explain when I never returned although I never saw Denise again.

When you called me last night for the first time in a year and wanted me to come to your tower like you missed the views newer buildings blocked now. The frames between each apartment's glass separated you and your neighbors into screens in the sky.

"I want to feel the back of your hands again with my fingers," you said. "I want to smell you again, to remember. Come here."

"I won't."

You called an uber to my studio on First Hill for the first time. I met you at the door and was startled: You had grown out your beard, but I had only known you as clean shaven. We listened to my records while we held each other. "Why were we never like this before?"

Denise went back to New York. I ignored your text messages. She ignored mine. I didn't realize yet how love worked. Your tech firm closed, I heard in the newspaper. I went to the same bar we met over and over again but you were never there. Not much about me changed as I went on my long walks.

It was winter again. This morning you left early—you never liked showering outside your own space and needed to wash your hair before going to breakfast. I walked in the crisp morning to Cal Anderson's dew-damp field where dogs played off leash and Seattle University students set up volleyball nets during the warmer times of the year. This morning it was emptier than I have ever seen.

My watch ticked fifteen minutes, a half hour, fifty minutes beyond the time you had agreed to meet. I sat on the wooden bench facing the cascading waterfall fountain and reflecting pool until the sun had dried the grass despite the cool chill in the air and I laid down in the loose dirt, limp blades.

I See then How I Will Die with Someone I Love

When the light bursts I will see everything.

Not everything around me: the white fire, dirt, shrapnel, men in uniforms and not, a stray dog, the caravan behind our tank, sweat-stained skin at an undershirt collar, innocent people outside the blast zone, innocent people inside it.

I won't hear anything but my ears ringing. I will see everything I have ever needed to know.

We open our eyes and it sears. This is how I knew when it happened. I sat up in bed and my eyes were burning. Let me say that this is nothing new, our body memory like laying in grass and opening up towards a white sky. Our body memory, the sudden bolt of light in a storm into our pupils. We open our eyes and it sears, and that is what memory is for us. Our bodies and our body.

Two weeks ago I sat up in bed and my eyes were burning in a different way. Something had dislodged in my throat and wiggled up into the space of my skull: the true memory. All of the boy and the girl selves together. The light flashed in front of my face and I could feel it go out. This is how I knew it had happened, that something terrible. He was not dead but the boy of us was no longer alive.

For that moment of waking I knew our entire life in the language of light. The room was too bright. All of the blood in our pounding inner elbows, ankles, carotid, throat. A taste of meat and the smell of sulfur. The clock ticking became unbearably loud and slow while my chest gripped me. Pounding, my ears. Ringing. Nothing was wrong, but suddenly flames engulfed our entire being. The inside of our mouth sweated violent and drool leaked in a trickle down our chin. The night breeze from the open window was filled with sand. We boiled inside and rose.

I didn't have time to run to the toilet. The vomit convulsed from me while I stood in the dim hallway. The girl of us, my entire body, convulsed in three spasms and red chunks oozed from my lips past the neckline of my t-shirt, dripping underneath it to my breast.

I woke up again in a slumped pile there in the hallway. Dawn had come, but it was a grey light. I had forgotten everything, but I knew immediately I was alone in the world for the first time in my life.

That grey light, like a morning when our bodies were six years old. The rain, it was Washington. We always woke up early, before Dad, so we had to wait in silence for the sun to rise and the day to begin. That always felt like an eternity, as our body had always been restless.

It was the girlself's idea. She was always bolder than our

boyself, who couldn't feel past the thick air of the house. She cut right through it even then, when we were so young. We dressed in our rain gear and grabbed umbrellas from the garage where we carefully, sneakily lifted the overhead door just enough to slip under.

The cloudy sky ripped open onto us. She twirled the umbrella, Minnie Mouse dancing with her. Wet strands of her thin hair stuck to her cheeks. We were soaking wet, our small bodies, almost instantly. He used the umbrella like a top, spinning it down the asphalt dock of our driveway.

The grass became a muddy river, and our boots became submarines. The rain did not stop or ease. If anything, it poured harder and harder.

We danced and danced. It was infinite, that time before morning, and it was ours. Together. And we believed that the two of us would never leave the pounding wet of that grey dawn. And we believed in the ways that we could always have each other.

The sun did rise, and it was a beautiful morning filled with the shade of light that only exists in the first few minutes of the day. My mouth was too dry. I did not have the energy to lift my one body from the carpet. The phone rang but I didn't answer. I was the only person who knew, it would take three full days before the Marines notified our family and had his empty body sent back to the states so it could lay in a more comfortable hospital bed.

We spent our childhood in Washington but it's not true: It isn't always raining. It's not a nonstop downpour. There's more of a moistness in the air, an accumulation of momentary drizzle, a grayness all around. There's nearly always a haze of fog hovering over everything shading in the sky and casting odd shadows on the treetops. The cloud layer does not always totally eclipse the sun with a thick film, but there usually are no more than a few holes of pure light piercing through the waxy cover.

This made that day, if for no other reason than the unusual radiance of UV rays, especially memorable. There was no fog, and there were no clouds. There was only the terrible brightness of clarity. How our body memory works, we found, is in these flashes of unbearable brightness.

The sun at noon in that cloudless sky hurt our eyes, so we spun in circles on the lawn. That way, we could look down both directions of the street. Into the sun to watch for Daddy walking home in his khaki uniform, and away to give our eyes a break from the brightness. We had not been in the sun like this since before we could remember. We were not used to it at all. That warm orb of early life was one long afternoon. It was beyond memory. Now, the explosion of the day's sun made us squint in an uneasy way because we weren't sure if we liked or hated it.

Down the street, up at the sun, down the street, down at the green green green grass. Down the street, sun, street, grass. Slam! The front door. In between flashes of street and sun and street and grass we saw our mother's legs pale in shorts descend the porch steps until they were just a part of the grass near us, twin tree trunks that grew gnarled and twisted.

"You two, stop spinning! You'll make yourselves throw up!" and laughter. She laughed like the white clouds they had in pictures of the past but not here, and the fluffiness tickled.

The boy of us giggled and spun faster, faster, faster. Girl

me, I did not. I stopped spinning but I did not laugh. Even then it was never simple. Street, sun, street, grass, streetsunstreetgrassstreetsun and sun and sun because he'd fallen backwards and the blades were cutting the back of his head. Light blinded his entire vision, and heat fell from the sky to soak into his body. This made him stop laughing. This made me, girl, laugh.

He could see nothing in the white orb of his sight, but he wanted Mommy so he reached and reached towards what was maybe a shadow of the tree of her.

"Mommy, Mommy! All I can see is the sun! Where are you?"

His hand found a meaty calf. Running down it was smooth. Running upwards the tiny hairs spiked into his palm. She laughed, so he did.

Rolling over he saw a calming yellow green. He closed his eyes and sighed into the darkness, exhausted by the wonder of the day.

I remember this. This half of us remembers this. Mom's face squinting in the sunlight, or because she was not happy there. The boy of us buried his face into the grass, and in the mist that is memory and the long sun-filled afternoon that is beyond it. The girl of us absorbed this heat and I vibrated up my throat into my eyes.

Our mother looked down at us for a moment. The girl of us was laughing. The boy of us was face down in the grass. Our mother got into her car in the driveway and left us. She drove away. This I never forgot, and I held it so the boy of us never had to.

HALVE IT

He never did remember as well as I did. I'm sorry. Maybe if he knew the truth the rest of our life wouldn't have been such a shock, but I loved how happy he looked in the sun. Maybe he wouldn't be here in a coma. Am I selfish? To take care of his half of me in that way? I know he did too, as much as he could. But now that we're here we can see how we both failed.

I can't stand to see him sunken into those thin sheets. The windows don't open in his hospital room, which I know that he would hate. He always hated the type of scent of antiseptic soap.

This is about a boy who is not a boy. This is about the boy who is not a boy wanting. This is about explosions of light.

About a girl who is not a girl. About distance. About never and always being alone.

I am a twin but I am on the other side of the world.

She is a twin but I cannot find her. I am afraid.

The twin of me is dead. Boy twin.

I look straight at the sun. I am not worried about it anymore. I don't care what that direct light will ruin of me. The white opening between my eyes and the sky above is miraculous and cleansing in the exact opposite way of rain. I suddenly feel the tears on my cheeks. Not that I was unaware of them before, I just ignored them. Fuck. All of it, words. Words. I didn't want to think about Jeremy ever again but my heart still pounded because it was noon again.

When I expect an extra bump of energy it doesn't come. I only feel something I'm not aware of. Nothing to think, say. Overwonder. The clouds, where are they? I lay still and finally closed my eyes because I knew the ghosts were coming.

No, the ghosts are not dead. The ghosts are bursts of light. I call them what I will, we call them ghosts but they are the most alive thing about us. At noon he always said the bursts of light inside our bodies exploded together. For the rest of the day we felt our slightly out of sync bleeding through our pores no matter the distance between us, but at noon bang bang, two heartbeats.

I hated when it rained. Girl twin. I was always fire. Call me Amber.

He is dead. Boy twin, rain, our mother's grey-blue eyes. Call him Jeremy.

It's always sunny in San Diego. Someone chose this as the place for the part of me that is him to die, as the other me looks out over the folds of blue with my feet buried in the sand. I look straight up from the beach chair's tan and yellow vinyl strips. I'm staying at a hotel on the beach because it was the easiest booking so last minute. Vacation is luxurious. The bikini-clad tourists next to me better be laughing while I cry because their job is to never think about funerals. I'll personally call security if I see an ounce of awareness in their eyes. I'm laughing though, laughing and crying because what else am I supposed to do with my dead twin brother's journal in my lap?

Sometimes I wake up on the ground after rolling off the cot, the dark of the tent and the heavy silence interrupted only by men breathing. I see then how I will die with someone I love. There will be an explosion. I know it like a memory although it hasn't happened yet. I'm looking forward to it the way I look forward to thoughts of my sister at noon, or the earliest visions of grass on a warm childhood day. I woke up like that just now and I can't fall back asleep. I don't remember that many details, but when the light bursts I will see everything.

In the spring, Dad was gone and we stayed on the ranch in Idaho.

The old railroad bridge was almost completely rotten through and technically not used for anything, but the county didn't have enough money to tear it down. It still stretched thinly across the river, the red of its iron flecking into the debris filled water and mixing with the clay lapped off the banks by the gentle current. Some sections were dimpled into large palm-shaped bowls that caught the rain. The water began to wear holes completely through the metal so that after a storm the bridge weeped slowly back into the stream.

We stayed down river at our father's father's old house, and on the weekends it always rained. We ran out in the early morning, woken by the pit pit pit pit on the window panes and ran, kicking the bloody mud with our heels until we reached the banks just west of the bridge. The vegetation laid flat under the deluge and we laid our two bodies on top of the grasses. Open mouthed and beside each other, the girl of us wanted to drink. The boy of us just gargled. The rain pooled in the bowls of our hands before seeping through our fingers and down into the earth.

By the time the sun fully rose and we had to run back before our grandfather noticed we were gone, the rain always stopped. The sky was always red at dawn, and then grey. We raised each other up onto our elbows, hands and knees, legs and the old railroad bridge sagged. It watched through its fingers as we ran again, this time away from it, us two becoming smaller and smaller and merging in the distance until there was only the idea of a new day with us in it. The bridge continued to oxidize and leak.

No, I don't know if it's still there either. Maybe we could have gone back there one more time, even if we know nobody who lives there anymore. Even if there is no father and no father's father. Even if there is no boy of us. Maybe I can go back there one more time, although there is only this, the me of us. I am all that's left.

The doctors pretend there is hope, but I know. We open our eyes and it sears. I'm saying this isn't new, our body memory. There's no way I could stand that hospital room for a single minute more and I know he can hear me better when I'm near the water. I know our boyself, is gone. I'm sitting in this chair waiting for everyone else to realize. Talking to my twinself. Saying goodbye.

The first lightburst. I don't know what else to call it.

They come when I least expect it, when I have nowhere to search but my own light.

The flickerflame of the Bic lighter cast a shadow of his head on the brick wall behind the bar. I could smell the stale Miller Lite seeping from his pores even before he set his eyes on me with that knowing smirk.

"Hey—"

"Fuck off."

The look on his face, wide open and surprised, settled on an angry grimace. "Bitch."

Eh, I've been called worse. The muted chatter and music from inside bled between us. Ke$ha, laughter, throbbing. I was certainly not in the mood to deal with a run of the mill douchebag tonight. I threw my butt down and pressed it into the alley with the toe of my boot and ignored him as he continued to glare at me from under the brim of his Rays ballcap.

It was a cool Tampa night and I was thankful for the breeze after working outside on the dock all day, one of the Friday nights a basic FSU sorority girl would shiver under a cute jacket from Forever 21. This guy had clearly mistaken me for one of those girls, as if I'd be flattered by his grunting hello on the patio behind Gaspar's. As if I wasn't miles out of his league. As if my wife wasn't inside waiting for me after I'd characteristically stormed off.

I did feel bad. I always felt bad—what a blunt use of words. Angry, sad, regretful, remorseful, pained. Bad, bad, bad. I could feel bad if I wanted to but it wasn't fair that I couldn't control my badness or that Charlotte often caught the edge of it, however blunt.

Inside, the dim light almost hid Charlotte's scowling at the bar. It was the first anniversary since we'd tied the knot secretly at the courthouse, both of us family-less and therefore embarrassed at the prospect of a wedding, a reception, a celebration of an empty first row at some non-religious wedding venue. She was stunning in her favorite black dress, its scoop neck and just-short-enough hem luring eyes from several men, delighting and frightening her. Her pale arms glowed moon-like and I couldn't look away. I'd ruined another night.

It was our first night out in Ybor City, or anywhere really, since our wedding. A lot had changed in a year. Three Hundred and Fifty-five days ago she started HRT. Today was the first day she felt safe coming out, and I ruined it by getting too drunk and gaining a memory I'd blocked for a reason.

"Finally, you're back," she said as I pulled up at the bar next to her. She didn't move her gaze or her hands from her vodka cranberry. The red shone in her eyes.

"Can we go home?" I spoke from my throat to stop from yelling again.

"No, I'm going to dance." She moved towards the strobing linoleum.

"I can't fucking be here."

"Then don't be!"

I grabbed her upper arm. "Please, let's just leave." I didn't mean to growl.

She brushed me off. When Charlotte made it to the dance floor a yellow light hit and her face transformed. Her lips and eyes opened and the split reflection from the disco ball checkered her cheeks. Some college guy in layered polos came up behind her and started grinding, and she grinded back. My blood rushed to my face. I wasn't even mad, just bad, bad bad again.

My body shuddered and the strobe blinded me. The people here were loud, their chatter and bodies rubbing against each other, and a whistling filled my ears. My head and neck grizzled side to side as my hand groped from the bar to the fake leather of the stool. I stumbled through the crowd, somehow finding my way out the door onto the sidewalk.

The nausea started in my mouth, leaked down my throat into my esophagus and stomach, then surged back up as I bent over and heaved all over the side of the building. I braced myself with my hands extended against the brick. Hot and acidic vomit spilled from my nostrils.

The breeze hit me. It was a violent awakening. The first ghost took over my body.

We were born. It was noon, C-section. Girlself first at eleven fifty-nine. Boyself next at the exact stroke of the highest sun. Don't you remember? I, boyself, remember this. You think you saved me from the pain of burning memory but don't you see that I saved you too? The first time we were torn from each other.

First, we were warm. When I needed I took from your strong body, and you gave. Still you were growing, and still I was growing.

Before language, sight, understanding we had light and sound. Remember our mother's voice from the inside? The first time we heard it was not with our ears. She laughed and our bodies vibrated. The first time we saw it was not color or shape, but pure light. We didn't have fully formed eyes but can't you see it now, that burst? Our mother cut open for us.

We were born early because she was sick. Our bodies were jaundiced and she sang about our yellow noses. The sound she made as laughter didn't feel the same. I reached towards you but my body could not move.

Our incubators sat side by side in the NICU. We wore knit hats and loose onesies. The slim mattress pads were lined with sterile sheets that smelled of diluted bleach and felt scratchy on the back of my head. I mostly comprehended fluorescence, the open air above the plastic womb. Side by side but apart we slept— what made us alive then? We felt the first empty.

My whole body convulsed. I couldn't open my eyes but I

didn't want to. I fell into the beautiful remembering.

I started this journal to keep track of these memories. I don't want to forget them again after repeating them aloud to myself for years. We arrived to the base a few days ago and I'm exhausted. I didn't have time until tonight to write but I know I have to: I saw myself doing this a few months ago in the light. I need to be powerful but all I can do is write my thoughts down. I know there is a reason.

The first lightburst came when I was six years old. It was noon and I laid on the grass in our front yard with Amber under a rare clear sky. The spikes of the lawn dug into the back of my head in a comforting way but I couldn't look up at the bright any longer. I held my mother's calf but then I was shaking.

The sheets rustled on our unmade bed. Charlotte sat on the edge to ease first one foot, then the other into her strappy stilettos. Humming to herself, she looked up to meet my eyes and smiled.

I wore a dress, too. It was a bright red and had thin straps. I hadn't worn it since the day we had met and it didn't fit me as well as it had eighteen months ago, but Charlotte had begged me to bring it out of the closet tonight.

"Aren't you excited?" she asked. The electricity I'd been drawn to when we met still excited me, but I rarely received that attention from her anymore. She sprang from the bed and loped towards me, grabbed my shoulders and turned us both towards the full-length mirror. My mouth curved into a smile as she massaged my shoulders. We looked like sisters even as I turned to kiss her cheek, her lips and our reflections lost themselves in each other.

HALVE IT

She pulled away. "Oh, I know!" she said while she strutted to the bureau, grabbed one of her red lipsticks and returned, leaning in towards her own face. "So we match, and people will know who I belong to." She made contact with her own eyes and puckered up.

I laughed and lightly held her waist. She tensed up at my touch: this was the most intimate we had been in months. A hint of dread rang into the left side of my chest and my heartbeat increased differently than before.

Charlotte and I fucked the first night we met. I went to The Honey Pot, the gay club in Ybor, alone to dance and not attract attention from guys. How ironic.

I didn't usually dance, but it was the night Anthony had thrown me out after nearly getting me kicked out of the Coast Guard, so I pounded enough rum and cokes that my body demanded to be moved, flailed, whipped numb and threatened to fall over. The lights that night were purple, blue, and red or seemed so as they hit my closed eyelids and illuminated my pounding blood. The dull chrome edge of the bar. Plastic streamers glimmering from the ceiling. Bodies, light and dimness seeping between them. On the crowded dance floor I saw spaces to slide my body into, places to hide. As I swayed the other bodies held me up and pushed me until I was in the center of them all.

I was dancing alone, and then not alone. She approached me from the front and grabbed my hands. My hips moved against Charlotte's. I felt her chest on my back, and her moist breath against my neck. She held me tight around my hips and for a moment I was still again.

I didn't need to be convinced when she whispered in my ear, "Come home with me."

We didn't leave her apartment for three days, and then I moved in.

Charlotte loved to dance but we weren't going to The Honey Pot tonight. She didn't want to run into anyone we knew. She wanted to go somewhere different, somewhere she would never have dared to go before. She stood up straight and looked herself up and down.

"I'm good, right?" she asked. I dropped my hands from her waist and stepped back as she gazed at her own furrowed brow. She took a deep breath, puffed out her chest, and smiled wide. I pressed my lips upward.

"You're good."

The first time was the most violent, the most unsettling. An energy like electric shock started in my fingertips, shot between my ulna and radius, vibrated my whole being without touching any of my cells. A knowledge that traveled in the nowhere spaces of me. I suddenly remembered the day Amber and I were born as if it were a dream. When I opened my eyes I was in my bed and our mom was gone.

We picked up habits to feel closer to what was missing. The red minivan she left us with still smelled like smoke and cinnamon. Boyself started chewing Big Red Gum. I started smoking cigarettes, the girlself of us. I liked the way the lighter sounded when the little flint caught, the lick of warm in front of my face. The sparks flew, shined, lit a stream of fluid at the pressure of my thumb. More than that flame and more than the sweet smell on my mucosal linings I liked the sound of small explosions. I liked the burning flavor of power as I took it into my lungs.

When the ghost gave me back my body, I was alone on the cold tiled bathroom floor. The brown puke had crusted over and cracked on my chest, stomach and the tops of my legs.

I called out, "Charlotte?"

No one answered. The house was painfully silent even as daylight streamed in from the window above the tub.

I didn't have another lightburst for years. I was afraid of them, didn't understand them. I still don't but now I trust myself. I think I know where they come from but must keep writing to be sure. They became gentler and gentler, more specific. Now, I can enter at will—not control them but call one forth. I never burst so violently again.

The second came on New Year's Eve 1999 on the turn of the Millennium, the day before our eleventh birthday.

"I hate Tampa," Anthony said.

He was exactly what you'd expect a douchebag from Connecticut to be. He was a Chief Petty Officer in the Coast Guard with a regulation haircut, wide eyes, teeth that glistened in the sun with the Bay. He was slightly above average looking, slightly above average smart, and totally average in bed. I loved him.

"I love Tampa! And New Year's is my favorite holiday," I responded with a smirk and slight whine in my voice.

I didn't even mention my birthday, which I'd dreaded since I was eleven. Eight years ago, but I wouldn't think about what happened now and ruin a perfect night. It was true, I did love Tampa even if I would never have chosen it. I'd never chosen a single thing in my entire life but I was young and hot, and I knew it. I'd pout a bit, suck in my cheeks and get what I wanted. Ha, it felt like my secret weapon—I never actually felt that way, I just used my face to make Anthony open his arms, his car door, his eyes. I didn't feel bad because I knew he loved the ways I could use him.

I've never written about this before. I don't know where I was when it happened, the immediate before or after. In my mind it's just a blur of light, smudged memory.

Amber across the table from me in a velvet dress. It was a late dinner, and Tonya's parents laughed at the head of the table. It was the first holiday season since her and Dad's wedding, so they flew across the country from New York. What was I wearing? I only remember my hands losing circulation while I sat on them, the needlepoints in my palms for a few minutes, the swelling, and the final numbness. I didn't want to eat. Overhead the stained-glass chandelier seemed to sway.

I sat next to Mr. Turner, Tonya's dad. He was short, skinny and upsettingly Italian in the way he spoke with his hands, emphasized the second half of every other word, and otherwise performed exuberance. He turned to me, making small jokes. When he touched my shoulder, the green of the chandelier entered me like a film over my eyes but I did not begin to shake. The film grew greener and thicker, and I saw nothing else.

We lived in St. Petersburg near the Coast Guard Station but it was too tiring for me with its flipped homes, yachties, and pristine Bermuda-shorted retirees. The house was in an enclave of houses full of Coasties, all men in their thirties with beer bellies, predictable Barstool Sports senses of humor, grunting laughs. I found them endearing but grating, of course. A couple of them were obsessed with me. A couple of them hated my guts. I laughed in all of their faces. I was friends with the only other enlisted girl who lived a few blocks away, but she stopped talking to me once I'd moved in with Anthony. Whatever, she was just jealous.

I basically worked, came home, hung around the same guys all day. When I walked around our block the smell was too clean, bleached under the palm trees. I didn't want to live in manufactured perfection. The Coast Guard was my living nightmare and since I got too seasick to go underway and had no aspirations towards any rate, I'd been an E3 for most of my career with no hope of promoting. Even getting one city over for the night was breaking free, a small crackle of what I might live after getting out.

"I know," he said, smiling at me and pulling me towards him.

He wanted to go, too but was just toying with me. His needy tendency to combat me was starting to bother me. I pulled away from the pressure of his hands on my upper arms, sticking my tongue out instead of kissing him.

The green morphed into shapes, people, a bed frame, the wall, grass, a pair of lips, Hot Wheels cars, Barbie dolls. Not a scene. There was no action. It encompassed me all at once with a lukewarm knowing, all of my body vibrating. The space around me shook and I became weightless. I liked how the knowing felt in my fingers, in my kneecaps. I was submerged in it, saturated by it. When I looked towards the surface of my memory it rippled and I squinted, swam up towards it.

Suspended in the layers closest to the sun was my friend Mitch, locked in time. I hadn't seen him since his Mom stopped letting him and Brianna come over, saying we were bad influences. She walked in on all four of us, them and me and Amber, in the bathroom with all our clothes off. Mitch had suggested it. He laid motionless now in the green current, his pale skin no longer glowing. I understood it all but was too young to funnel it into words.

I swam in the green for the rest of the night and missed the ball dropping.

New Year's Eve. We ran around the house after dinner, both ourselves. The house curled around itself, the living room opening into the kitchen, into the dining room, into the entryway, into the living room. The floor had green carpet that was coarse on our soft soles. I know Jeremy didn't remember, but I do. I always hold the worst memories.

He sat very still after it happened. He didn't remember what it was. He wouldn't run any more. There was a new millennium episode of SpongeBob on the TV and he sat criss-cross and stared at Caveman Patrick. We pulled the bottoms of our t-shirts through our necklines and danced like Britney Spears. I laughed but he didn't. I knew everything was wrong from the way he turned his head to the left when Dad called his name.

The next day we turned eleven. There was no celebration. Tonya told us we had misbehaved the night before, that her father saw it. We stayed in our separate rooms in our pajamas all day.

I did kiss him. That was love, anyway. His clean-shaven

face hurt me below my lips.

"Let's go babe!"

Anthony dug his fingers into my arms for a few seconds, then let me go.

"Charlotte?" I yelled, frantic as I peeled myself from the floor.

I knew I'd fucked up. Charlotte wasn't there. I didn't mean to actually leave her at Gaspar's, but I couldn't remember if I had. The splitting ache in my head expanded to my chest as I tried to remember past spewing all over the sidewalk.

What could have happened to her. My brain spun.

I ran to the kitchen, still completely naked. I slipped right before the counter and caught myself on the cold laminate. I was dizzy, out of my body. I laid my head down on my forearms, the ulna pushing into my face, the hard but blunt edge of it in my skin. Metallic and tangy, my own arm made me shiver.

I looked up and scanned the kitchen frantically, and I saw it. The post-it was stuck to the toaster with *I'm safe but I can't do this* in Charlotte's cursive.

Inside of us craves knowing. Having inside of us. Becoming full of. Our selves yearn to be of something else. We want to be had, contained, held although nobody can own us. We cannot be totally encompassed by another, only in light. We cannot erase the lives we have lived. We can't explain holes in memory or fill them, discover what is lost. No ways of knowing. Only aching in our lungs throbbing with our airbound veins.

When the ghost came into me, girlself, I lost control of my limbs. I felt it first deep within my hollow organs. Then, in the marrow. Now at the tip of my fingers, which moved without my meaning to. I held my own cheeks the way a beloved would hold them, a mother would hold them.

She didn't need my permission but I said, "Take me away from myself."

It was like looking directly in the sun and realizing the most important secrets of the universe as they burned under my skin. It wasn't a concrete memory that came to me as she straightened my back and pulled me from the side of the building, but a wave.

I didn't want to be a Marine. Hell no. But they said I couldn't do it, so I ran away and did the damn thing. I didn't want to be in the Coast Guard either but at least as a Marine I'd feel useful.

Obviously, it wasn't for that patriotic bullshit, it was matter of course. I don't hate the Middle East. I don't want to kill anyone. Everyone loved America then. It was only five years after 9/11 and we lived on a military base. It was the only choice. I had no follow up questions.

The funny thing is even as Tonya called me faggot, too much of a bitch I didn't even understand what that meant. I was just an empty shell when I was seventeen. I had emptied all of my memories into the lightbursts. I didn't feel happy or sad, only hungry for anything else. Amber had no choice but to enlist in the Coast Guard, they forced her to do it when they kicked her out. I wanted to at least make some choice, have any power. I signed my name and didn't look back.

My vision didn't get blurry, I just got angry. Charlotte watched me transform, just as she had so many nights before. I didn't want to dance, which is all she wanted. I wanted to sit right at the bar.

The memory came with the anger. I didn't dare say it aloud.

My jaw clenched. I felt my posture change but I couldn't stop. I was in too deep, and I felt an ache under my bottom two ribs. My breath exhaled out of my teeth. Charlotte turned to me and I saw her smile turn into a wince.

"I can't stop—"

"Not tonight."

I shrugged her off. "I'm going out to smoke."

I closed Jeremy's notebook and the wind blew a bit of sand in my mouth. It was all too much to handle, his writing and my memories. I hadn't heard from Charlotte in a week, since I got the call that Jeremy was here in the hospital in a coma and I flew across the country to be by his bedside even though we hadn't spoken in five years. I was my twin's only family and he is about to die. I can't stop myself from laughing even as tears tunnel down my cheeks, into the corners of my mouth, and into the cuts I bit on my lip until it absorbs the salt in the air and stings.

Cutoff

The Businessman came in and sat at the bar. Derek inspected him like a cut of lamb left on the butcher's counter.

He put his briefcase down. Derek imagined it was filled with Manila envelopes held shut with metal clasps, blue and green filing folders, and very important documents bundled with oversized paper clips. Stocks. Accounting invoices. Inventories. Loss statements. Standard Operating Procedures and miscellaneous but steadfast protocols. Spiral-bound guides to salesmanship and leadership style manuals. Long lists with neatly calculated bottom lines. Clean thoughts that fit in careful forms must be what filled his head as he sipped a Maker's Mark, neat—a drink most of the regulars would throw back as a shot.

Derek didn't play the pull tabs anymore. He no longer pined for attention perched on a barstool. Now, he came in nearly every day and coiled in the corner booth closest to the door away from the artificial lights, the thrill of a quick glance, and the other men who paid him no mind. The mid afternoon sunlight refreshed him as it snuck in the small window in the door, slatted by the half-drawn blinds.

He nursed his beer and watched the bar until someone caught his eye. He'd learned that nobody came here this time of day to be *with* each other, not really. The regulars came to sit across from Food Network on TV and feel the space expanding between them like heated mercury. The Businessman's pinstriped suit was new but he was just another man beneath it, after all. He'd entered their rituals of communal solitude.

The Businessman shuffled his freshly shined black leather shoes that glinted even in the dim resting on the brass support at the bottom of the stool. The diamonds on his watch face gleamed and his hairy forearms peeks out from his pushed-up sleeves. An overcooked layer of perfection charred over his wide chest and broad shoulders as if waiting to be pierced and peeled back with a fork. First bite.

He must be traveling to the city for a very important client meeting, Derek imagined. It had gone in an unexpected direction most would assume was failure, but the Businessman always succeeded. He retreated here to strategize before returning triumphant with the solution that would win him the client, the contract, his birthright.

When he was young, before he grew into that knack for crunching numbers and began carrying leather-bound cases filled with paper trails any lawyer could defend, he must have been in love. He drove a pickup truck on the potholed roads along the Oregon coast, worked in the fish processing plant in Newport, and spent his weekends with his wife and son watching the waves retreat during low tide.

They took off their shoes. Their toes sank into the damp

earth on their special beach, the one only locals knew about. First date, proposal, midnight rendezvous. It was at the end of a cul-de-sac on the North side of town. He carried the toddler down a trail in the woods in one arm and held his love's hand to guide her. Under the grey sky the brown sand expanded, but the cliffs contained it. The beach did end, and in fact was only visible when the water was all the way out. They had to time the visit with the tides. He always had a sense for the ocean, where it was going and when it would come back.

The ocean spray and salt wind mixed with the drizzle. His grin and easy laughter didn't tell what he already knew. She was in love with his best friend, had been for years. A corporate job opened up in the office so he applied and got the gig. The world turned. The tide was coming in. Their son giggled as the waves tickled his feet. They all smiled despite their secrets and headed back before the sun set.

After the house was asleep, the Businessman loaded up the pickup with his scarce belongings without leaving a note. Through the windshield wipers he saw a bear in the sky anchored by the North Star. The road passed above the rocks where water covered the exact spot he had held his son, watched his wife smile just hours before. He rolled down the window with the crank lever and spit over the edge.

As he drove up the coastline, the new Businessman let himself feel angry for the first time. The sharp pain in his chest widened to vibrate through his whole chest and he discovered a tight ball of sadness below his bladder. The warmth shined in the base of his skull and sinuses. Before the tears came out he pressed into the center of the steering wheel as hard as he could so the car emitted a blaring, aching honk for as long as he could stand.

The Pacific to his left was empty, so it did not echo. It wasn't too late but he had made up his mind. He would leave all of this behind.

Derek broke his reverie. Whatever old life the handsome man wearing a Double Windsor had was none of his business. Cloud cover had shifted, turning the light through the blinds a shade too bright. Squint. It was time for another beer. He scrambled out of the booth and staggered up to the bar.

"*Jii alxcluioh a;lsdkfjp owieurilahsndf,*" he whispered to Jerry behind the bar.

"Oh honey," Jerry cooed with an inflection that showed how much he really cared. "I hate to say it but you've reached your limit for today."

"Mmm. *lxclaieohasdflj asodifalshdfowie.*" Derek sauntered back to his booth to contemplate.

The Businessman closed out, adjusted his checkered tie, and picked up his briefcase. He laughed a bit at himself for carrying it around; he'd been fired the day before but the irony of bringing it with him to drink whiskey alone made him feel better. On the way out the door he smiled and winked at the drunk leaning on the table near the exit.

Something about the gleam in his eye or the plaid shirt he wore reminded him of his father down in Oregon.

Peel

When Holly gazed into the reflecting pond, the ducks sauntered away from her. How lucky she'd been to receive all of the best advice. She had taken the day off to relax in the park. The ducks' feet disturbed the underwater so slightly the surface didn't even show. The clouds and the sky shivered.

A couple sitting on the bench held each other. They were young, maybe early twenties. She wrapped both her arms around his denim jacket-clad shoulders. One of his lanky limbs fit loosely around her waist. What a crime, young love. Holly both missed and didn't miss so easily being with someone, that melting.

She went back to laying in the grass with her grey hoodie bundled under the curve of her neck. Not amnesia—there were always things she could not forget, the slither and scutter—but a presence that demanded her current attention upwards to the cirrus clouds streaked in the spring's warm sky. The gloom cracked beneath her sacrum and the pressure lifted.

It had been settled. She wanted to visit the garden, but

the police had torn it down. The section of Cal Anderson that once thrived was guarded by chain link. Near the trees, a dandelion burst like yellow flame. It was almost spring and the weeds always bloom.

From Holly's tote bag: an orange. One of those totes with a distinct design a company thought a person like her would want to show the world about her personality. One of the GMO oranges bred to be large and easy to peel. She dug her nails in anticipation of the white layer of pulp before the juice.

A flash: The last time she saw him. Those green eyes simmered in the back of her mind, or were they hazel? It had been long enough now that the memory dissolved into the droplets of pond water flowing off the ducks' green and brown feathers. What had she done with the letter opener?

Underneath: Packed dirt, firm Earth, a newly laid layer of sod that hadn't grown in yet. The edge curled slightly upward. Her fingernails caught, slightly bending. Holly wondered whether the curve of her keratin or the delicate roots would give first.

The pat smooth surface was now disturbed by dimples and loose topsoil. The sheet of vegetation clung where the blades had entered deeper. Only the small yellowed section that failed to root parted from the ground, risen scab. A roly-poly scurried from the light into the underworld of damp flourishing life.

Her orange sprayed juice droplets that fell onto her face underneath. She held the fruit directly above her head and let the pieces of peel fall around her, creating her own personal solar eclipse.

Wedging her thumb into its flesh to tear off a wedge felt

familiar. Holly's fingers remembered and delivered the wet, acidic strings across her lips and into her mouth.

She had started at the corners of his eyes. Across his cheeks. He had opened those woman's love letters with it, and she had found them. Holly's throat remembered a flash.

She'd loved oranges ever since she was a girl. Once they'd come here, to the grass at Cal Anderson where unleashed dogs ran and let strangers pet them. He had set up a picnic blanket and unpacked cheese and champagne from a cooler. An orange.

What had she done with the letter opener? The light in the interrogation room was as bright as the sun. Her fingers were still caked in his blood. The one-way mirror behind the detective reflected her green eyes, the wet streaks in her hair. She did not respond.

When she was a girl, Holly's father took her to feed the ducks. They brought leftover Wonder Bread that was no longer good enough to make sandwiches with. He taught her how to cut the bag carefully with a Victorinox pocket knife and use her fingers to break the hard crusts. Together, they threw the chunks as far into the reflecting pond as they could. The flock would glide to the center of the disturbance and remove the evidence: Feeding the ducks was a crime.

Everything changed after her father died of Covid. She couldn't even visit the hospital to say goodbye. There was no memorial.The deepest layers of her being curdled and each corner of body ached. She laid in bed in the studio apartment she shared with her boyfriend. The rest of that time was a blur, then a flash. She remembered everything.

The letter opener had an ivory handle and a silver blade

that was sharper than one might expect. It always lay on the table next to the door, where the bills and coupons and handwritten correspondence from friends sat. Holly's father's. He used it to open the letters he'd carelessly left beneath a spam credit card offer and a message from the Washington State Department of Labor concerning her ongoing unemployment benefits.

When the police found her, she was lying on top of his body. The neighbors had complained about a broken window, the sounds of a struggle, and an uneasy atmosphere. Instead of bringing her to the hospital, they put her in the back of the cop car and then into a cell. She didn't tell them anything because she was still in shock. The shards of glass had left cuts on her forehead but luckily didn't leave scars.

Her boyfriend's face had been cut open with a small blade and the skin was peeled back down to the throat. He wasn't breathing by the time they arrived on the scene. Nobody could quite piece together what had happened so there was nothing to prove. The police never found the weapon. How lucky she'd been.

She sat up now. She didn't want to dig underneath the sod, destroy what was trying to grow beneath her. There were several more dandelions peeking their golden heads all over the park.

Holly was content. It was going to be a good spring, she could feel it.

Room 119

Ollie walked steadily towards the Willamette River with his hands reaching towards the creature's serpentine neck and head rising from the water. The dawn fog had only just settled and the chill of early morning bit at the top of his ears and shocked his lungs for the first half of each inhale, but not enough to numb the churning want that ground his ribcage. It had been a long night.

The river creature's green scales caught the first gray strands of light and shone like the yellow eyes that locked into his gaze. "Closer, closer."

As Patrick drove into Eugene hours before, the sun drenched itself and went out. In early spring the days stretched longer each day but once the dark settled around the trees and rumbling SUVs 9:30 pm was the same as midnight. First once a month, then a single night a week, now every few days he drove into city limits and sent a Grindr message: "I'm almost there."

He pulled into one of the many motels whose red Vacancy signs glinted in the drizzle. The clerk at the check-in counter barely looked up as he checked in under a fake name.

HALVE IT

"Room 119."

Knock, knock.

The twenty-two year old's skin caught the white parking lot lights that splashed around him as he stood in the doorframe. Pale and thin, he writhed and made hissing noises when he was supposed to.

Typically Patrick and Ollie didn't speak; the ritual of their care no longer required voices. Their embrace immediately quenched their mutual ache and wonderful delight tingled from their spines. Musk and chewing tobacco mixed with oat milk and allspice between their flaring nostrils while yeast and spearmint swirled into their wet mouths.

The thirty-seven year old's chapped lips were soothed by the boy's smooth tongue and split by his bites. The door shut, plunging them into the damp dark as they staggered to the bed, taking turns leading and resisting each other.

"Ollie, we have to stop."

Afterwards, Patrick's first whisper aloud since February sliced the tender yearn off their exposed bellies. They were laying arm next to arm, moist with sweat. All he could let out was a soft moan that reached to his toes.

"The judge finally decided. I'm going to see the girls again. We have to stop this. If Clara found out, she'd use it to take them away again." The moment he'd been waiting for had finally come and a few of the pieces that had been missing from his chest had been reinstalled so that the twenty-two year old was too tight a fit.

All the blood pooled in his stomach. It was expected, after all. The night always ended and they both went back home to their individual sadnesses. Ollie cleared his throat before he silently rose, slid into his boxer briefs and Carhartt pants, and left with the door thudding softly behind. He pretended to walk the long way home—he had no intention of making it there until the morning.

When he reached the asphalt path in the park, a familiar stirring in the water caught his attention.

The creature swayed with the night breeze as it beckoned. Its underside faded from emerald to a blanched color along its underside. Ollie wanted to run his hands along the whole length of it and feel the rush of the current around him while he wrapped his arms around its thick skin.

The starlight still faintly poked through the rising light like the creature's eyes. Together they would make their own constellations. He'd held onto hope—that the love he felt was real—since he was a boy. Whenever he felt desperate he would end up here with his longest friend. He believed in the creature more than he believed in the men who held him for a few months before their universe shifted and there was no more room.

Patrick didn't stay the night. It was time to forget how he'd made it through the trial, the long months alone without purpose. One message to send, a memory left on the bed. He hoped it was going to be the last time. "Come back."

Back when they first met, they'd gotten a bite to eat at the Dairy Queen.

"Did you ever hear about the Willamette River Creature? I'm the only one who ever sees it but it's always been my best friend." Ollie sipped on his vanilla shake hard through the straw.

Cream too thick to swallow caught in the tube and he laughed.

"You'll have to show me next time." The thirty-seven year old dipped his fry into chocolate. "I'd really like to meet someone so important to you." They smiled together.

No one had ever wanted to meet the river creature before. "He's shy. I don't know if he'd trust you."

He didn't say, "The creature only comes out when I'm alone. I'm not alone because I'm with you. I don't want to see my friend ever again if it means you never leave."

He said, "No, I don't think you need to meet it. You're more important to me than the monster."

When he made it back to the motel he didn't need to knock because the safety deadbolt held it open a crack. There was nobody but a small stuffed animal from a bar's claw machine left in room 119. A green and yellow serpent.

Ollie didn't cry over any of these men. They were always the same but he still loved them all. At the end he always turned back into a snake, slithered away. When he held the token Patrick had left to his chest he felt the same as when they were together but more at peace since the desire had left. It was its own escape to no longer reckon with the man's body, his unspoken need. The shades kept out the growing light, the covers kept him warm, and everything was safe.

There were only a few hours until check out but he was so tired. It had been a long night. He snuggled with the fluffiest pillow and what he hoped was the final last memory. Exhausted and alone again, the twenty-two year old took a nap.

Manifest

The leftover chill's talons lost their sharp once the rain stopped. Miriam sat outside on the steps leading to her front door watching her new neighborhood.

The morning was loud with animal noises as a neighbor's chickens cackled. She didn't pray any more because she no longer believed in god or goddess, just the Universe. The robins in the persimmon trees by the gate shrieked and fluttered amongst each other. Runoff flowed down the edge of the street and poured into the sewer grate as the clouds began to break.

Just her luck, within the week of searching on Zillow the upper level duplex in Georgetown was hers. Sure, the thick panels of glass didn't completely shut out the buzz of descending planes circling the municipal airport and the yard needed some fresh grass seed, garden shears, and a lawn mower cord pull but the newly remodeled kitchen and year-old carpet was just what she'd asked for. The empty smell of a new beginning vibrated in her home.

Miriam just about willed what she wanted into existence once she decided it. Although she always stubbornly clutched her single minded determination, her Taurus ambition didn't play a role in this; she faithfully trusted that the Universe would present her with exactly what she'd envisioned sooner rather than later.

It was time to prepare for her day. In a few hours Mother would buy her a new piece of furniture. From her perch on the stoop she created a mental inventory of everything that she would fill the space with: a leather sofa larger than the Wayfair futon tucked in the sitting room corner, a matching ottoman that flipped open to store Pendleton blankets, a golden framed mirror hung above a cherry wood side table in the foyer.

When she arrived at the antique furniture store, Mother was already waiting.

Endlessly reliable and detail-oriented, she shocked her youngest daughter when she left out her typical greeting. "You're slouching." Miriam longed for the familiar pang that hit the middle of her chest, the sudden straightening of her spine, the anger and sudden movement. She wished the four years since they last saw each other at Grandma's funeral were nothing.

Instead, no words. Mother looked her up and down, taking stock of her shoes, the pleats in her plaid skirt, the slight rise of her crop top above the waist and its neckline at her throat, the brown eyeliner she wore, and whatever changes in her facial complexion needed to be accounted for.

As Miriam crossed the street towards Mother, she imagined the diamond tennis bracelet slinking around her wrist like an earthworm as she sipped a vodka martini. The layer of dirt beneath those French-manicured fingernails showed when she didn't bother to hide her disapproving laughter. Today she wore a safer smile than Miriam remembered.

Her grandmother had retired in Florida, the opposite corner of the country where her elder twin sisters had moved after graduating from the UW and marrying six foot tall, blue-eyed cousins who worked on oil rigs in the Gulf. They'd met when they were summer stewardesses on a National Geographic cruise up to Alaska and the men were engineers. Miriam spent that summer in the woods writing poems, meeting temperamentally gentle boys whose future careers in academia never provided the beachside life that Cynthia and Phoebe savored.

When Mother stepped out of the air conditioned airport in Miami the humidity weighed strangely. She'd never visited while Grandma was alive. One regret. Her eyeshadow curdled.

After the wake, Mother drowned in her grief at the hotel bar. She'd stayed on the West coast, of course, with the law firm she built instead of a marriage. Another. She reapplied her lipstick—too much had been left along the martini glass rim.

"You know why couldn't we get along, Miriam? You always reminded me too much of her—too witchy and unrealistic. Look at you now, alone again. You'll never get what you really need." She tapped the drink and threw her head back with that terrible laugh.

Miriam flew home from Florida alone in a window seat with a wish and two strangers in the row. She couldn't remember what she muttered under her breath all those years ago as the plane lifted into the air, but she knew in her heart it had come true as she hugged Mother closely. Their bodies were softer now and they molded into each other's missing pieces.

The store was filled with old knick knacks, vintage toys, half-lit neon, and decades of Playboys wrapped in shiny plastic sleeves. None of the furniture fit the vision she had focused on that morning. Mother didn't speak, so she also remained silent.

When they came to an oak hope chest her eyes lit up. The interior was lined with green velvet and the lid was carved with an intricate nautical design. It was unlike anything Miriam had ever imagined. She hadn't known she wanted it, but Mother knew. She purchased it and still only shared silent, meaningful glances with her daughter. The delivery was arranged by the clerk.

The hope chest arrived at the duplex the next morning right as a private plane was beginning to land. Miriam sat on her stoop looking from the unkempt grass up to the sky and back down to the runway she couldn't see past a dozen rows of houses.

It wasn't what she wanted, but it's what Mother had been able to provide. It was enough, it was enough. It was beautiful in its own way. As the moving men carried the heavy piece of furniture into her home and set it down at the foot of her bed, she knew again that the Universe would always give. Many of her memories confused her or left something to be desired, but Miriam did not have any regrets.

Her favorite part of the flight was the end, when she knew the wish she made during take off had been safely left in the heavens. When she returned from Grandmother's funeral, she decided she would never pray again.

Perpendicular

Aaron and Steve had just returned from their latest vacation.

All of their friends wanted to hear about it—so badly, in fact, that they got roped into the couple's position in the front half of the Pride block party line. Every detail of the trip was so engrossing that a group of first 3, then 6, then 12 people grew and Damien began to wonder if they'd ever move forward toward the entrance or if the line itself was the main engagement of the evening, if catching the bleeding echoes of faraway DJs and sipping to-go cocktails from A Pizza Mart were the same as tucking into a corner inside the gates, if the watching people passing towards the back of the queue or catching the edge of a conversation or leaving to find someplace with a shorter wait was the same as floating with the crowd who made it into the party.

Then all at once the line moved forward a whole block. People came and went in waves and the bouncer counted up and down with an electronic clicker.

"We just got in this morning! From Iceland!"

"The geothermal hot springs ... "

"No, surprisingly even on the foggiest days it wasn't too cold."

"You have to go to this little place in Reykjavík we found at the end of an alley."

He liked to listen for a bit and then stare into space. He'd split a joint with some people on the way over and the hybrid mist vibrated from his chest, down his legs, and into his brain making him smile.

They didn't tell their friends that Aaron had twisted his ankle the first day they arrived. It was their first hike, and right where the main road turned to gravel he'd stepped too much on the outer edge of his Merrell boot and the loose rocks shifted under him. Most of the vacation had seen him laid up with rest, ice, compression, elevation, ibuprofen, anger, boredom while he scrolled his phone and reposted the stories Steve tagged him in as he explored the glaciers, countryside, and city on his own. The itineraries were already booked and paid for, better not to waste. Tonight he stood unsupported and in pain.

They'd been together for just over a year now, not that Damien could tell. They finished each other's sentences. They wore matching button up shirts from Express and the same brand of jeans. When they laughed together, Steve turned his head to meet Aaron's eyes and they harmonized.

In every relationship Damien ever been in, the one-year mark is when it became clear things weren't going to work out; that's when the unforeseen tripwires appeared and the inevitably misplaced foot triggered internal alarms, self sabotage safeties, protective booby traps in his mind. Seeing the group of gays gathering around the perfect couple made him feel at odds with them. Some weekends their lives intersected in these lines but otherwise they grew endlessly in disparate directions. It was for the best, then, that he was alone for six months after Meredith left.

Then you arrived in his DMs three Tuesdays ago, handsome: dark features, classic jawline, full lips kept smooth with frequent spearmint balm applications, unwrinkled forehead that read perpetually unbothered and content. You lived in your own reality, your own perspective. Of course you did. You were over six feet tall. Damien was glad to stand silently with you behind the crowd clamoring. The line moved twenty feet closer to the party's entrance.

The chatter from people waiting and the dance bops from the DJs swirled with the usual Friday night traffic sounds. Steve couldn't stop thinking about the dick pic you had sent him the morning before the trip. He saw it first thing while checking his messages and brushing his teeth—so exact in his routines. Did he like it? You never heard back, but the message was marked seen. You smiled to yourself because you loved to kick the dust.

The world whirred around you, cross faded. Murmurs and laughter from people you'd known for years, some you'd met once or twice, a few that you loved for a few weeks at a time but no longer spoke to for no particular reason, many that you only waved to in passing or chose to ignore most of the time collected in the air with a pulsing beat underneath it all. Was it like this last year? Will it ever be like this again? If only you could comb through the sounds and the people who made them, smooth and straighten the evening into a flat gravel road you could walk barefoot over without tripping over.

Damien grabbed your hand, then let it go. He was too stoned and lost in thought, always watching everyone around him with those hazel eyes, usually in the corner of a dim bar or the edge of the rooftop party. He didn't like to be alone. It had been a good time getting to know him, sitting with him at Deluxe and watching him eat chicken wings and drink non-alcoholic beer.

When he was happy he grunted and exclaimed, "Scwha!" in an adorable burst of joy when a flower, a sudden realization, a dear friend entered the room. Sitting in those moments was enough. Damien inspired you with his quiet and sincere delight, even if they never lasted very long.

The line moved forward again suddenly. "Not too much longer! We'll be in the next group, for sure!" Aaron said. He was excited to get in so he could find a place to sit down; his ankle was killing him and he felt the limp coming on. Steve wrapped his arm around his waist to support him instinctively.

You didn't want anything in particular, but you hated waiting. A sharp turn cracked in the center of your chest. There were too many things that needed to change. You turned to Damien, kissed him on the cheek until he met your gaze.

"I think I'm gonna go." He nodded. You didn't text to let him know you'd made it home.

Halve It

Darts (12)

Ten years ago, I only watched the men play darts. I didn't know the rules or any techniques so I found my corner of the back room, waited for them to notice me, sat nervous and silent with my slitted eyes slanted towards their feet.

Now, I cross my legs near the dart boards as the usual guys throw, laughing when their bearded buddies hit the twelve three times. I look up at my friends playing halve it. I know the rules but I don't drink beer any more or join their games. I'm quiet still but in a different way: The men I love like being overheard. I watch them from the corners of my eyes and listen instead of hide.

None of the stories are the same but all are the same sort of almost-true. Every time they are repeated, they warp a little at the edge or the locations change but the heart stays true.

They become the versions of themselves they show off to impress each other. When they describe good memories—the times they won at pull tabs or when they took their sons fishing in Alaska for the first time—their buffalo nickel eyes shine. When they murmur about seeing their ex on the dancefloor weeks after they broke up or spraining their ankles on the first day of vacation, they stutter exaggerated nonchalance but their shoulders tense up, betraying them.

When I used to come on Tuesday afternoons, before I knew what the regulars drank and what days the pool sharks claimed the table, Jay noticed me.

I wasn't observant because the world frightened me, the people in it. Knowing them. Throwing pieces of me into the air between us and waiting for the tantalizing, undeniable throbbing that expanded from an arrow back to the chest, pang.

"Wanna play?" Jay's deep voice hit my sternum. I wanted to play so badly. "I'll teach you everything." He had brown eyes, a permanent flush to his apple cheeks, and a wide pink mouth that broke easy into a smile.

"Alright." I became a version of myself I could give to him, puffing out my chest and cocking my head to the left.

When he laughed, though, I melted.

Today they keep the score. That day we didn't.

"First, just try it." Jay watched me miss the board completely three times in a row. The bile of my young anger, a boy's inexperienced rage out of control in his own body, rose from my stomach as I clenched my teeth. He saw me and he knew.

"No, buddy. It's fine. Just try again."

Feather (13)

My first boyfriend Diego and I walked through the Arboretum holding hands. It was a wet spring full of rhododendron blooms. He was slightly taller than me, which made his arm over my shoulder and mine around his waist seem natural.

We both had the same green ball cap from Filson, but mine was smeared with grease and his was sunbleached.

The thin branches curved over the path and the sweet smell of fresh leaves, moist earth, and pollen called to us. When it started to drizzle, we sat under the canopy and held each other.

There were no birds, only signs that there had once been. An empty nest collapsed above us. A chirping song bled in the distance.

In our boyish love we learned to hold each other, or to let ourselves be held and to embrace another.

I found a red feather and stuck it behind his ear before I flicked his earlobe with my tongue.

"I'm going to keep you forever," I whispered and ran my hand across his chest, grazing. His strong fingers massaged up my spine to the back of my neck as he whimpered under me.

The wet seeped into our pants. He pushed my head down gently until I squirmed, looked up at him from his lap. The fun was in fighting back, using our muscled bodies together.

We growled and laughed our lean frames against each

other as we wrestled across the path. His hips pressed into mine. We coiled open.

His teeth dug into my right shoulder when he bit me. I shrieked, pleased.

I lost the hat when I moved last year. Stayed out of the Arboretum for a long time after we stopped speaking to each other—he didn't want a boyfriend, after all.

The last time he sat in my apartment we didn't touch; the distance between us transformed us into men.

Sometimes I wear red and remember. I do remember.

Armpit (14)

The UW law student buried his face in my armpit.

I was hands-and-knees on his bed with a straight spine.

He kept trying to get me to relax, but I couldn't stop giggling. My abs firmed up and my body curled. He smacked my ass to shock me out of myself, which worked for a moment.

His meticulously groomed beard against the tufts of hair that had just begun growing.

I brushed my teeth as I scurried past the lawns from the light rail station to his house because I wanted to make a good first impression. Since I was already out, I hadn't had time to go home and shower or put on deodorant. Thankfully the CVS near the Capitol Hill station had a travel brush and paste for me to use, waiting until I returned to the dark to spit.

The fountain at the top of the promenade gushed as high beams of light aimed at her face caught her best angles.

My wrists chafed under his tight grip, both held by one of his hands near the headboard. They'd be red tomorrow.

The bedroom was neat with freshly vacuumed carpet lines, IKEA bookshelves stocked with science fiction classics, two monitors and a gaming PC atop the otherwise clear desk, and a tucked-in ergonomic chair. One empty water glass on the nightstand stood next to a vintage radio alarm clock that showed 1:28 AM in red digital letters. I brushed a Pikachu plush from its resting place by the pillows.

We Snapchatted every so often for a few years after that, but never met up again.

The law student saw me out, walked me to the door quickly. The rest of the house was not as clean; there was a pile of dishes in the sink and a pair of wafting gym socks on the sofa. He kept the secret parts of him ready for me to see.

I don't trim any of my hair. I don't use beard wax. I put off haircuts as long as possible. But I shower every day and rub a mix of rose water and essential oils behind my ears, on my wrists, in the hollow of my throat, in my armpits.

When his coarse tongue hit the deepest part of my furthest corner, I surrendered. All the tension in my shoulders, lower back, and hamstrings leaked out of my muscles and I let him touch me.

When I reached the next streetlight, I turned around and he was still there, resting his hands on the top of the doorframe as the streetlight across the way illuminated his bare chest and underarms.

He inhaled me, sucked the worst out of me.

I got to keep everything that was left.

HALVE IT

Teacher *(Any Double)*

After showing me how to grasp the dart with my fingertips gripped lightly just behind the sharp point, Jay stood behind me to show me how to throw. Steel tips. He guided my right hand with his and rested his head on my left shoulder, showing me how to aim.

"Relax and breathe. It's supposed to feel good when you release it." With his breath in my ear and his calloused palm around my knuckles, I let go. My first dart on the board.

Tender *(15)*

I was addicted to the first time.

I found A. at the bus stop in front of Hilltop Red Apple when we both took the 60 to QFC.

B. found me in the corner of the Cuff during Wednesday karaoke while he sang something by Selena Gomez.

D. and C. always had their eyes open for a third and I smiled at them while I passed their porch on a summer afternoon.

Sometimes it was an accident. I wasn't expecting to find E. in the SeaTac Terminal D bathroom before my flight to Oakland.

Sometimes it was on purpose. I was hoping F. would come ask what I was reading in the Ballard Brew Hall at the end of Terminal D at SeaTac before my flight to Guadalajara.

I got a room during Boy's Night at Steamworks. 29 and under got in free. I met G., H., I., and J.

Nobody made me feel the way I felt with the law student, that release. I wanted to be tenderized again, to want to give someone myself again.

I gave D. and C. another shot at Portland Pride because they let me stay in their hotel room. Embassy Suites downtown has a hot tub, unlimited free drinks and popcorn during happy hour, and a fireplace in the lobby. K., L., M., and N. all slept in the suite with us.

O. was my neighbor for about a year. He lived in a close friend's spare room for cheap and was always the life of the party. The second, third, fourth, fifth, sixth, and seventh times were fun but I still couldn't give him what I wanted him to have.

We went out on Halloween with his girlfriends, him as Batman and me with a lazy cowboy hat and button up I called Indiana Jones. It was almost good enough, but I couldn't let go of my search.

Sometimes it was set up for me. My friend thought P. was perfect, so we arranged a meeting at the bouldering gym for some competitive flirting with a beer after. We sat in the sauna for a while before he slipped off his towel. But P. was too perfect for me to relax around.

Q. had to be it. I was so tired of looking, but he didn't shower everyday and smelled terrible.

R. let me live in his house for a while, but I never stopped paying my apartment's rent or got a U-Haul.

After that I was alone for a while.

Rib (16)

Jay just wanted to play darts with me. I just wanted to play darts with Jay. It was nice.

We met every Tuesday before the trivia crowd took over the pub. We'd order a late lunch of Chinese food—spare ribs, pork fried rice, egg flower soup.

"Watch your posture. Don't slouch."

He was retired from the Air Force and worked part time at the grocery Co-Op down Madison to pick up extra cash and meet his neighbors. He spent some afternoons here, if not with me then with whoever was playing darts that day.

"Like a pen. Like you're writing something. That's how you hold it."

Jay didn't touch me again after the first time, but watched carefully as he coached. His voice vibrated in the exact tone needed to make me listen like he was moving my body for me.

"The ribs between the numbers can't crack. Slide between them and hit the one you want."

Usually nobody else was around. Occasionally the barback Alan watched, brought us refills on our Diet Cokes, or wiped tables.

"Close your left eye. Then aim just a bit too high first. Then lower."

I imagined him briefly wrapping his arm around my ribcage like the first time he taught me how to aim. He held me for just a moment but then let go.

We didn't talk much about our personal lives but enjoyed sitting in silence together, watching each other play. After a few games the crowd started to build up and I would leave him for the evening. I don't know what he did when I wasn't there.

"One throw, fluid with a follow through. Commit to it."

His quick bits of advice hit me, shattered between my ribs. I sucked them in so that my body would absorb them to use without my mind. Shards of what he told me shattered, circulated from my chest into arms, fingers, calves, toes.

"Just a bit behind the line, knees bent."

I aimed, threw, and hit the inner bull's eye.

"Great! Now you know the easy stuff. Go practice."

Healing (17)

Diego called my name.

At Diesel in a crowd of people, all O.'s friends.

Every now and again my old neighbor and I ran into each other, remembered the fun feelings we had together, and felt them again. I lost myself in a cloud of ecstatic gin & ginger ales.

When would the tabs close so we could go home?

Diego called my name with a question mark at the end after walking across the bar to say hello, reminding me that I was daydreaming in public again.

Or was my drink too strong?

I couldn't hear him clearly. He said his sister's name

and smiled.

I hated that I knew his sister's name. She'd always been amazingly sweet and dear. I cut his whole family off when he hurt me because I was young, just a boy. I let all of them in because I was. Let's be real, I wasn't trying to deal with all of that drunk at Diesel in front of O.

Diego was skinnier now, had a different lilt to his voice. It took me a few moments to recognize him until I realized it was his red T-shirt from Cha Cha Lounge.

"How are you?" The emptiest question. I didn't even want to touch him.

"I'm good, here with," I gestured vaguely in the general direction of O.'s friends.

"Are you still...?" He did say something about my previous career, friends, life but the music played louder than his voice.

"No, not at all." I didn't offer any further details.

He took a few seconds to look at me. He was clean shaven, now. I looked at him too, but didn't feel anything for him. "It's nice to see your face," he said.

I couldn't believe it was true. I never thought of him any more.

"Yeah, you too buddy." I smiled a bit and nodded, which I'd become very good at doing since I'd known him.

As soon as he left I turned to look for O. because I didn't want Diego to think I watched him walking away.

Shatter *(Any Double)*

After a few months, Jay stopped showing up on Tuesday afternoons. I didn't ask around.

Alan watched me play darts by myself for a few weeks, then I stopped coming too. I ditched my Diet Coke and started drinking Manny's beer.

Back Room *(18)*

Jay and I played darts in the back room.

S.'s mouth tasted minty in the back room. Orbit gum.

The giraffe was too tall. His head knocked the top of the doorway entry to the back room.

I sat at the table with a view over the whole bar from the back room with T., the manager of that new Italian restaurant on the Hill.

At midnight Sunday night, U. came over and asked for a kiss. I played coy for about 20 minutes teasing him but yeah, I kissed him in the back room.

On blacklight night we all covered ourselves in neon body paint and fluorescent temporary tattoos of animals. The Lion roared. The back room quivered.

I taught V. how to play darts, but he was naturally better than me and I got mad.

I taught The Scorpion how to play darts, but he was terrible at it and I got mad.

HALVE IT

The bartenders put the stools up in the back room an hour before closing but W. went back there anyway. He was kind of an asshole.

X. spilled three vodka Redbulls on the back room floor. He swung his arms when he laughed and he laughed often, infectiously.

The Horse had thin long hair in a ponytail. When he came into the back room, he only wanted a hug.

It was in the back room where the grocery Co-op employees had their quarterly outing with pitchers of Rainier and popcorn. Y. grabbed the seat of my jeans and let me eat a few slices of pepperoni pizza.

The Platypus brought his mom to the back room.

The Turtle was changing his career. He showed me his college essay in the back room.

When I brought my laptop to the back room, The Panda asked me what game I was playing. Then he wanted to know what I was coding. Instead of telling him I was writing I went home with him.

It's a great room, but most people don't make it past the bar and the pool tables.

I don't even come up here that often any more.

When Z. smiled at me in the back room, I ignored him.

Halve *(19)*

I looked it up tonight on Facebook and the UW lawyer didn't become a lawyer after all.

He's writing Science Fiction stories and teaching classics in Chicago.

My buddies Charles, Jonathan, and Wade are here in their corner. Maybe I'll go say hi to them now. When I knew them before I drank too much. I'm excited to see them again.

I keep tabs on everyone when I can. It helps to run into them, like O.—he has a boyfriend now.

Alan left for a while, then came back as a bartender. He wanted there to be a dragon in this book, but I solemnly informed him that there was already a river monster.

The credits are about to roll, buddy.

I'm typing on my phone at the bar thinking about everybody that I love. Isn't it lucky to feel so much love?

We played a game of darts and I didn't hit every time.

We played a game of darts and you did really well. I've been watching you, too.

Everybody's doing the best they can.

The Scorpion rules the back room.

The Lion manages an event venue up north in the mountains.

The Turtle is so sweet and has everyone feeling so safe with his care. He chats at the bar.

No one's seen The Horse in a while, but I follow him on

Instagram. He's making art in Santa Fe.

I finally asked around about Jay. He moved back to Spokane to look after his mother. He didn't come back.

I decided to stop drinking a week ago.

No more chasing the first time.

I'm trying to pay closer attention and get to know people better so I can tell who played each song on the jukebox.

Everyone's always around, except the people who moved or died or changed their lives.

It's time for me to change my life.

Mirror (20)

I look up from washing my hands and he's at the urinal.

There are a few more grays in his hair than I remember and he's lost some weight. Been going to the gym and it shows in the bulge of his bicep. A new haircut.

As he shakes off I call his name. He turns around with a blank expression.

"Do you remember me?"

No more words. We've been at this game for a long time. The music outside the door bleeds with exuberant chatter.

I'm not the same as I was ten years ago. Some wrinkles. My back hurts. I want to lay down more.

What advice would I give my past self? Laugh more. Don't take it all so seriously. Say I love you more. Wave at strangers. Don't be afraid of caring about them.

The man zipping up his fly looks like my dad.

The bathroom antiseptic and piss scents mix together into the comforting smell I've come to love.

I won't say his name. We've moved beyond that type of knowing. I don't ache to be seen or even touched by him.

Watching him in the mirror above the sink, I shut the tap and grab a paper towel to dry my hands. He's not impatient with a warmth to his face that didn't used to be there.

If you want something, ask for it. Work hard at the things that matter—love, friendship, family—and let anything unimportant fall away. Be loyal, honest, and frank.

Hold people when they're with you but remember that nobody stays.

I guess I've been staring at him too long.

An annoyed expression flashes across his face and he raises his eyebrows before he smiles again.

A line is starting to form behind him and across his forehead.

"I'm sorry but no, I don't remember you. Maybe next time I will."

We only see what we want to see. Look around and you'll see yourself everywhere.

Stay quiet about your delusions so they last longer.

"Sorry, must have thought you were somebody else."

Again *(Inner Bull's Eye)*

There is so much I still do not know, even though I keep trying. That last part is almost true.

There's no use in lying. I don't know everything, or anything even. I only know the easy stuff.

Forgiveness *(Outer Bull's Eye)*

There's a new kid sitting in the corner on Tuesday afternoon. He's blonde with a little hoop in his right earlobe. When he smiles, I smile back before his eyes flit back down to the ground.

"Hey, buddy. Want to play?"

An Interview with Joe Nasta

When did you start writing and why?

This question always makes me laugh! Once, in a poetry workshop in Williamsburg, the teacher asked us all on the first day how long we'd been writing poems. We met in his apartment and opened bottles of wine. Almost everyone said they'd been at it since they were young; such dedicated students! When it came to me I confessed that I'd only been writing poetry for two years. When he scoffed, I couldn't tell if it was admiration, disgust, or amusement. Not that I cared what he thought.

Yeah, I wrote a few stories here and there when I was younger and always wanted to be an author, but I only started studying writing after I finished my engineering degree in 2015 and had time to begin my independent journey. I was always more interested in writing fiction, but at the time poetry workshops were easier to find and enroll in—even in New York, many fiction workshop groups required manuscripts that were already written. Most of the poetry workshops were more generative and a great place for someone with less official writing education to begin. I understood the value of training my ear, technical eye, and poetic sensibility. I love beautiful sentences more than anything! My craft education is as a poet with special attention paid to narrative forms, long poems, and the relationship between the speaker and the reader. I'm forever grateful to the poetry teachers who offered these workshops and the people I met in Brooklyn.

My prose education came on the West Coast during Corporeal Writing workshops in Portland, Oregon. There I learned how to unlock my core metaphors, allow my writing to flow freely from me in whatever hybrid forms it presented itself as, and the power of generative revision. There, I discovered the true power of storytelling: to create a connection with the reader, hold up a mirror, and send them a glistening gift. I wanted to show the reader a beautiful and powerful stone, polished and glimmering with truth. There, I learned to write beyond rage, anger, vengeance and return to the essential question we all face as writers. What do you want to give the reader? How do you want to make them feel? In a world filled with sharpness, I want to give my readers warmth, safety, care, joy, compassion, and tenderness.

Sprinkled through were other workshops at Hugo House, open mics and slams in Seattle, collaborations with peers and friends that allowed me to break through to deeper levels of craft and storytelling. Every step of the way I got closer and closer to uncovering my mission as a writer.

JOE NASTA

Why do I write? Why does anyone write? My mentor told me he could only go so long without it before he became miserable. For me, I need to redefine my reasons for writing at the beginning of each project. For this project, I wanted to tell mystical stories that cut straight to the heart of an emotion the reader might see themselves in.

Which authors or books or media influenced you the most as a writer?

I'm a sponge. I'll absorb any media I interact with, which is useful and dangerous. I'll begin writing and see traces of something I didn't even remember being influenced by! So my process when consciously working on a project is to define what pool of influence I want to draw from.

While I'll always be influenced by the writers I've studied with or admired for years and years (Lidia Yuknavitch, Alexander Chee, Porochista Khakpour, Joanna C. Valente, Jack Kerouac, to name a few).

In the year leading up to this project and during its writing, I focused on reading the following short fiction collections to prepare:

A Good Day for Seppuku by Kate Braverman

Holidays by Lisa Ruffolo

Sweet Talk by Stephanie Vaughn

The Lover of Horses by Tess Gallagher

Brief Encounters with the Enemy by Saïd Sayrafiezadeh

The World is the Home of Love & Death by Harold Brodkey

The Collected Stories by Leonard Michaels

Everything here is the best thing ever by Justin Taylor

HALVE IT

Earth Angel by Madeline Cash

Nights from this Galaxy by Will Weitzel

To varying degrees, I was influenced by these books and authors.

While writing each story, I also used my initial drafts as a jumping off point before asking myself, "What archetype, universal story, myth, or legend can I see just outside the margins of what I've written?" I then researched media relating to that and used it to inform my next draft and revision strategy. After finishing each story, I looked up keywords on Spotify to find a song that I wanted to tie to it as well—this sometimes led to me changing the title!

I'm constantly influenced by the people around me, things I observe or watch, places I travel to, music I hear, living writers I pay attention to. As a writer, I try to stay in conversation with as much as I can so that my work is in relationship to the people and things that are important to me.

Which authors or books or media had the biggest impact on you as a person?

Here's the meaty question! To be impacted not just as a writer but as a person—that's the goal not just as a writer but as a citizen, a friend, a human being. Kind of scary to answer honestly. I'll make a list of what comes to mind and not say much more. I think influences like this come in phases and change with you, so it's not that deep to me. As I said, I'm a sponge and am constantly being influenced by new things. These influences are maybe more foundational and will continue to affect me I think.

Jack Kerouac and the Beats. Jack Spicer. Alex Dimitrov.

James Schuyler, John Ashbery, Joe Brainard—the whole New York School. Lidia Yuknavitch, Domi Shoemaker, and the whole Corporeal Writing community. Gary Paulson and Lemony Snicket. The internet, especially Instagram and TikTok over different eras on those platforms. Poetry slams back when they were super popular. Random movies I watch and the special memories I make with people when I watch them. Lana del Rey. Queer masculinity. Classic American tattooing as iconography, like Sailor Jerry and Ed Hardy. British and American sailors, sea stories and shanties and diaries—John Masefield and Richard Dana and Samuel Coleridge. Internet alt lit and autofiction from the 2010s.

Which of your original twelve Prompt stories are you most pleased with?

I like the first one, "The Winner." It was the start of the journey and helped me set the main setting for a bunch of the stories as well as the tone. I returned to it often when crafting some of the later stories. I wanted it to be a touchstone for the first three-quarters of the book.

Which of your original twelve Prompt stories did you find the most difficult to write?

The one about the twins, "I See then How I Will Die with Someone I Love." It's kind of autobiographically-inspired, as many of the stories are. But this is the most personal one.

Writing or sharing art is a little sacrificial in that the writer needs to leave some of their own blood to lure in the reader.

HALVE IT

This story is that for me. While the other stories focus on others, this one is mostly about myself.

It's the culmination of many years of trying to write something and nail it down. I think I finally succeeded and am excited to leave that story here in this collection and have it be a part of this project with Blue Forge Press. That's why it's the longest story in the book.

It's also right at the center and distinct from the other stories. It still fits with the kind of story you might overhear someone tell at the bar. It's definitely the most ambitious piece in the book.

What book on writing do you recommend?

I was most impacted by Edward Hirsch's *How to Read a Poem*, so I recommend that. It's shaped my tastes as a reader, but also my approach to the writer/reader relationship. He's also my grandfather in poetry, ha. I love following lineages of mentorship and influence, which I think is important and holy.

More than books on writing, I recommend investigating the lineages of writers you admire—who they studied with, where they published, who their colleagues and peers are—and studying those works. Read their craft essays and apply their perspectives to your own work. If they offer workshops, take them. Go to their readings and meet them if you can. Send them (respectful) emails.

What advice would you give an unpublished writer?

My advice is less about publishing and more about creating a sustainable writing practice and building a life as a writer. Lauren Groff once tweeted something about how everyone, even her husband, had to reckon with writing as this big rock in the center of her life. That impacted me and the way I thought about writing—dense, unmovable, heavy, and the main focus of every choice that I make. You have to decide if you want that, and then allow yourself to do it.

Obviously, there are other priorities like family, employment, health, and friends. Step one is to decide how big this writing rock is for you and the role it's going to play amongst everything else. Is it a boulder that everyone needs to reckon with? Is it a pebble that you playfully skip in the pond of the art and writing community? Is it a pumice stone that you use to massage your lovers' feet? Is it a fossil you use to explore your past in private? All of these are great roles writing can play. Knowing this will help you decide if you want to publish and how you will. Liska Jacobs told me at the 360 Xochi Quetzal residency that she knew many great writers who didn't publish at all; they write and share their work privately and that was enough for them.

Step two is to keep writing. Even if it's not for a story, poem, essay. Freewrite or journal. Think about words and how you use them, even outside of things you would consider publishing. Connect with the joy that writing, storytelling, and language brings you because that's what's going to ensure your writing continues to be an important part of your life. Publishing is nice, but it's not what's going to give you satisfaction long term.

Step three is to read widely and engage in community. If you want to publish, you need to understand the landscape. If you want to publish and make money, you need to understand the market—which is totally different. Meet people who also write and engage with their work. Check out journals both online and printed. Go to in-person open mics/meetups. When you do publish, realize you're being welcomed into a larger group of voices—find out what you like and how you fit into the writers around you. When you do this, you'll know where you want your work to exist in the world and where it will be embraced.

Step four is to learn. Actively seek out new resources and ask for help. Take workshops. Learn from mentors who want to work with you. Share work with peers. Accept and offer feedback gracefully. There's always more to improve upon, even if you're done working on a piece.

Do you have a "dream project" as a writer? What would it be?

All of my projects are dream projects. I'm a Capricorn so coming up with an idea, creating a plan to execute it, monitoring my progress over time. Creating lists, checking things off. I've been doing this for a long time.

What's hardest is the space between your intention and vision for a project and the reality of what emerges on the page. When I was first starting out, my skill was not measuring up to what I wanted to produce by a long shot. It was frustrating but I learned that this difference is always going to be there. In the process of writing, the project changes. Unexpected ideas come up and the vision shifts. Even as I develop more skills, and even if I was able to execute my plan perfectly, what the project wants to be is different than I ever could have imagined. Being okay with this and letting go of what I expect out of a project has empowered me.

I'm excited to finish this collection and move forward towards whatever my next dream project is. Maybe a collection of Friendship Poems. I'll have to go walk around the woods for a while and think about it. See what comes up!

Your stories will be published in a set of Prompt collections with the other Third Generation authors but also as a collection of just your own work. Did you have a conscious theme for your personal collection?

When I first started this project, I did not have a theme. I was confident I had the tools to use the prompts, generate my own portals to work through them and fill pages, revise and hone the stories I wanted to tell in a month's time. However, I had no idea what the stories would be about and let my environments and personal life experiences during each month help shape what I ended up writing.

And what a ride. I became a regular at a gay bar. I moved. I broke up with my boyfriend. I changed jobs. I returned to places. I eavesdropped. I made new friends and lost old ones. A lot happens in a year, but underneath it my favorite themes and places emerged: the bar, the woods, destinations I visited.

Most of my stories were short, and I thought about why. It was hard to produce longer stories in a month's time! But I wanted to use the constraint in a more meaningful way that contributed to the book's craft and thematic elements.

Many of them relied on archetypes and somewhat vague rememberings that sometimes lacked excessive details. Once I wrote "Hard at Work" about the barback eavesdropping as he passed from group to group at the bar, I realized that these were the type of story someone might tell at the bar that he would have overheard. Maybe there's details missing, and maybe they're a little rushed. But the core is simple, honest, pure. I wanted these stories to capture that energy. This all circled back to the recurring setting of the bar.

I wanted most of these bar stories to be like a dart throw, short and hitting a different spot on the same board. The voices circle in the room, but they're together. Some familiar characters pop up in different ways, and over the year I took aim at different emotions and experiences. But each month I showed up and wrote a story about care, love, friendship, family, experience, community. The stories are about continuing. Trying again and again even when you fail or miss the dartboard.

By the time I reached the end of the 12th story, I had a clear vision for the final one. 13 stories. The dart game Halve It has 13 rounds. I knew I needed to write something that captured that part of the collection's theme and craft, so I endeavored to write about Halve It and the act of showing up for yourself over and over in love and life with a form that mimicked the rounds of the game.

Who do you write for and how does it drive you to create?

I write for myself and for my friends. I don't think that much of a wider audience but trust that when I write with care for the special people in my life, the tender emotions I try to express will still come across. When I'm writing and dear ones come to mind, I try to put myself in their shoes and figure out what would make them smile if they read the story. If they saw themselves reflected even slightly, what remembered details or angles would make them feel good or seen? Everyone wants to be seen. I want to give that satisfying recognition to readers.

By starting with the people I know, thinking about what archetypes or greater stories might appeal to them, then pressing the details of my story into those molds with my hands like putty, I remove the excess material and polish the surface with a glaze to create a glinting object that I hope catches a reader's eye. If I achieve a wider audience, I hope they see themselves in my characters and feel seen as well.

It's an art to write so carefully. Over the years I've experimented with serialized fiction online that buried these details and memories, sometimes failing to imbue the necessary sweetness and nuance. It's hard work to learn and practice this! Just like any other way of relating to people or communicating with them. Now, I always try to return to the essential goal of giving a warm, loving embrace to the readers, my friends. When writing the stories in this collection I tried to find the sharp teeth and lip corners of characters that reminded me of my friends and invert them into dimpled cheeks.

Most of my writing is this whispering. I'm not necessarily looking to be widely published or known by strangers. I sit in my corner murmuring. Come visit me and listen for a while, and I'll tell you what I remember or see in you, lovingly. Or you can listen to me talk about somebody else that I love and I hope it makes you smile!

The drive to communicate care, to entertain, and to embrace my special friends in writing is why I write. It's a lifeforce and a reminder. We're all here together in community and we all give each other what we can. I have some stories. I have beautiful words. I have my little mirrors and stones I can wrap in brown paper to give away. They're trinkets for everyone I meet. Making these things for them is not just driving me to create—it's what brings me joy and drives me to continue being alive.

Optimally, we're always growing and improving as authors. Talk about how you grew or changed as a writer over the course of creating your stories for *Prompt: The Third Generation.*

This has been an amazing year of growth for me! This is my first time delivering my creative work on deadline, communicating regularly with editors, and working with a publisher so I've learned a lot about being a professional fiction writer and what that means. I'm excited to use that knowledge to continue developing my skills and use them even more in the future with bigger and bigger projects.

This was also an opportunity to hone in on my process: How exactly do I go from a blank page to a full story in a set period of time? I had my strategies for generating ideas and writing, for revision that I brought with me—at the beginning of the year I was confident in those skills and excited to use them! However, showing up every month allowed me to translate that into a repeatable process that I can continue to develop and use to regularly write high-quality work. This will help me work on my own projects and deliver contracted creative writing to editors and publishers in my professional life.

I also had the opportunity to experiment a little with narrative form. It can be difficult for me to write a direct narrative that follows a timeline; I usually envision a strange shape or angular action (like hitting a cue ball to break the racked up pool balls, or the rounds of a game of darts, or moving through a room and eavesdropping, or the stream of consciousness of a concierge with head-jumping POV) and try to imitate that. Playing and practicing, and sometimes trying to write a more straightforward narrative, has definitely helped me grow.

I'll keep saying it, also: Just showing up and being accountable over and over again has helped immensely. Meeting a deadline. Being with the page. It's been a great year.

Imagine the perfect cover for your personal collection. Describe it... even if it's impossible.

I have a couple of ideas for the cover that are pretty similar. The first is: black. Just a dart board on it, but not hanging or anything—just floating in space. Maybe a young guy shirtless holding it. I actually found a stock photo that could be an inspiration. The title and my name in letters like a neon sign, maybe in slightly different fonts, red and white and green lettering.

Or, like a creamy white cover. Just a dart board hanging on the wall with some darts in it. Roundish font like a vintage ad. A kind of dusty haze over everything. Red letters. Like some of the CLASH Books covers—I love their designer so much!

These are just jumping off points. Maybe a commissioned illustration in a comic book/video game character style. Maybe a collage of different elements like the cover of The Novel: Poem by Paul Hoover. I'd like to get playful and explore possibilities. The best designs and art are usually found in the process.